BREATHLESS

~~The Beaumonts~~

Angie Daniels

Caramel Kisses
Publishing

THE BEAUMONT SERIES

Caramel Kisses
Publishing
Caramel Kisses Ink
www.caramelkissespublishing.com

DEDICATION

To my husband Todd Christopher Wilson
I can't breathe without you.

To all of the readers who have fallen
in love with the Beaumonts,
this story is for you.

BREATHLESS

~~The Beaumonts~~

Angie Daniels

Caramel Kisses
Publishing

Prologue

BOOM!

Seven guns exploded simultaneously. Once…twice…twenty-one shots.

Senior Master Chief Keith Falcon stood at attention alongside other members of his unit. United they stood, faces grim and emotionless like the honor guards now shouldering their guns. Together they had served, fought, and protected their country. And now they were saying goodbye to one of their own.

Silence swept over the gravesite as the chaplain stepped forward with a bible in hand. Before he could begin his eulogy there was a high-pitched scream and then heavy sobbing. Keith's eyes shifted to the grieving woman, standing in front and then to the two Navy petty officers, struggling to keep her from collapsing onto the coffin that had been draped with a large American flag.

This can't be happening. There's no way he's gone.

While the chaplain spoke of integrity, valor, and honor, Keith stilled as he remembered the sailor who'd lived his life according to the Navy's core values.

Honor…courage…commitment. It was because of his faith, allegiance, and Master Chief Derrick Webb's selfless dedication that brought them all here today, to say goodbye.

Chaplain Smith's voice continued to boom over the sobs from Webb's family and friends.

This can't be happening.

He can't be gone.

A heavy sadness descended upon Keith like a smoldering blanket. There would be no more shit-talking. No more dart tournaments at Mickey's Bar. He would no longer be able to hear that obnoxious laughter which sounded more like a squealing pig. And he would never get a chance to break the tie after they both earned ninety-nine points during their last fitness exam. Instead, he was there to say goodbye to a sailor, and a good friend.

"Present arms!"

Keith saluted. His mind was in turmoil as a bugler sounded taps and the flag was lowered.

"Order arms!"

Keith swallowed the lump in his throat before he could bring his eyes to focus on Webb's fiancée, now seated in a chair in the front row. Somehow, he had managed to stand tall and composed, yet the muscles at his chest contracted when Sedona cried out again in sorrow. As his commanding officer began the ritual of folding the flag, Keith thought about the couple.

Sedona was all Webb had ever talked about. The two were supposed to have married upon his return. Unfortunately, because she wasn't his wife, she wouldn't receive any of his death benefits. His mother would. Keith clenched his jaws while he watched the officer walk past Sedona to present the folded flag to Mrs. Webb.

The rest of the ceremony was a daze, but somehow he made it through. Once Webb's body had been lowered into the ground, Keith did an about face and headed toward his car.

"Falcon, wait up!"

Keith turned and spotted another chief running up beside him, wearing an identical dress blue uniform. He was grateful for the distraction and focused his attention on his curious eyes and freckled cheeks.

"Hey, several of the guys are going over to Mickey's Bar for a small tribute before we head out. Wanna join us?"

Just yesterday their commander had ordered the entire unit to take three days mandatory leave. He shrugged. "I might stop through for a minute."

Johnson nodded. And at the distant sound of Sedona's heart-wrenching cries, Keith remembered.

He still needed to deliver the letter.

"I'll see you later," he mumbled then started back toward the gravesite. The crowd had begun to thin. Mrs. Webb was standing beside her husband, talking to the chaplain. He had already given his condolences to them at the church. His eyes then shifted to Sedona still sitting there staring down at the ground as if hoping Webb would resurrect like it had all been a dream.

He'd give anything for that to happen.

Keith loathed having to make his next move, but a promise was a promise and he was a man of his word.

Shoulders back, he moved stiffly over toward Webb's grave and Sedona Beaumont.

Chapter 1

Three years later

"You are living in a no-win society."

"A what?"

Sedona leaned forward on the chair, making sure her client could hear her through the speaker phone. "A no-win society means even if you're trying to do everything right, someone will still judge you negatively. If you go left, you'll be judged for not going right. If you do nothing, you'll be judged for not doing something."

Hailey Child blew heavily into the receiver. "So what do I do?"

"Break the rules," the life coach replied matter-of-factly.

"I don't understand."

Sedona stroked the gleaming oak conference table as she explained, "Hailey, you're trying to decide between attending a regional conference that would mean career progression, and attending your granddaughter's college graduation." Glancing down at the client file in front of her, she continued, "Did you prepare the list I mentioned during our last session?"

"Yes, I have it right here," she replied eagerly.

"Okay, then let's hear it." Sedona leaned back and crossed her legs beneath the black pencil skirt as she waited.

"Well… first off, if I don't attend the graduation, my son and granddaughter will be disappointed. Graduation is probably one of the most important days of my family's life. Family is everything and I should always put them first. On the other hand, if I miss the conference it could affect my next promotion. I should feel honored to have been selected. I may never get this opportunity again."

"Good, now keep going," Sedona urged.

Hailey spoke up quietly. "I already promised my boss I would go and represent the corporation."

"Nice job. Now where's the pushback?"

Hailey whistled low and long. "I'm torn, angry, and afraid."

"No, those are emotions. When you feel it, stop, and write them down. For example, if I don't attend my granddaughter's graduation, she will be hurt."

"Okay."

"The thought of hurting her makes you angry. You may realize that sometimes hurting people cannot be avoided."

"So true," Hailey mumbled.

"The same goes for your job. This may be a once in a lifetime opportunity. That's your emotions telling you no job is worth missing an important family event."

"This is tough. I…" her voice trailed off.

"Don't let it be." Sedona shook her head even though Hailey couldn't see her. "Write it down. As you go through one thought after another, rationalizing, you will see that you're responsible for your own choices. You can't please everyone, so make decisions that feel right for you."

"You're right." Hailey's voice became clearer. "I see what you're saying."

"Making choices can be frightening but they can also feel empowering, independent," Sedona said as she swiveled her chair to stare out the window behind her. "After a while you'll find you care less and less about how others judge you and what ultimately matters is how you feel about you and the choices you make to shape your own life."

"Hmmm, you've given me a lot to think about."

"I'm glad to hear that. Well, that's our time for today," Sedona said with a half-smile on her face. "I want you to write down your feelings and we will re-explore on Monday." She stayed on the phone long enough to put her appointment into her calendar, and then shortly after ended the call.

For the next few minutes, Sedona jotted down additional notes about her client, noting where the session ended so she would know where to pick up the following week. A moment later, she put down the pen, pushed away from the conference table and rose from the chair. Walking over toward the window, she gazed outside at the amazing view and sighed.

She had bought the waterfront colonial-style home in Hampton, Virginia just for the views of the Chesapeake Bay from all of the rooms at the rear of the house. Not to mention the small cottage in back that she had converted into her business.

After earning a double-major in women's studies and psychology, Sedona spent five years as a psychologist before she began craving more personal fulfillment and decided to become a life and career coach. She spent most of her time doing motivational speaking engagements and coaching professional fortune-five-hundred corporations. But her passion was coaching people who wanted to enjoy professional success and a more satisfying personal life. In the last year, Sedona felt as if she was finally making a difference in other people's lives.

"You asked me to remind you about dinner at Bone Fish Grill tonight."

Sedona turned around and faced her assistant who had just stepped into her office. As her words sunk in, Sedona blew out a long breath. "Oh yeah."

"Would you like me to cancel?" Energi asked and swiped a finger across the screen of her iPad, ready to access her personal calendar.

"No, there will be no need." Besides, her assistant wouldn't have found a phone number associated with the appointment because there wasn't one. "No, I'm going. A girl's gotta eat," she replied and headed toward the door. "Speaking of food..." She hadn't eaten since breakfast and was feeling a bit too hungry to wait until dinner. She signaled for Energi to follow her then exited the cottage. Sedona moved across the raised wooden plank path that led through a rose garden toward the rear of the main house. Lush grounds surrounded the property. The garden was one of the reasons why she had fallen in love with the house. Fall was almost over and no roses were in bloom, but the foliage was beautiful just the same.

"Don't forget you have a nine o'clock conference call in the morning with Laverne Grace," Energi informed her while trying to widen her steps and keep up with Sedona's long strides. She often forgot that at five-ten wearing four inch heels, her long legs sometimes made it hard for others to keep up. "And then a teleconference at three. Oh, and Jennifer Cason is still waiting on a confirmation to the invitation for their annual holiday conference at the convention center next month. They have allotted time for you to do a book signing following the event."

She hated last minute invitations but Jennifer was a friend of a friend, and with her business just kicking off the ground the last thing she needed was to make enemies. "How's my schedule look that week?" Sedona asked, turning her face into the light breeze flowing from the bay.

While they strolled across the yard, they went over her calendar. Energi jotted down notes in the iPad and chimed in when needed. Her schedule was booked solid for the rest of the year and Sedona was grateful.

"Maggie called from St. Martin's Press. She wanted to know when she can expect the synopsis for your next book."

As she climbed the steps onto the deck, Sedona pressed her lips thoughtfully together. She was scheduled to release her second self-help book next year, but was still undecided as to which direction she wanted to take it. The first "Living a Satisfied Life", had hit number one on the *NY Times* Bestseller's List for eight weeks straight.

She turned around and looked down at Energi who was waiting patiently at the bottom of the stairs. "Tell her I'll have something for her next week."

"Got it. I'll see you in the morning."

Their work day had ended and the twenty-four-year-old marketing major was off to class. She waved as Energi continued around the path to the driveway at the side of the house where her car was parked. Sedona walked across the large white composite deck to the French doors and stepped inside. She had three hours until her date, so she reached inside the fridge, retrieved a handful of grapes and popped them into her mouth, then sighed.

Why do I even bother?

For the last six months, she'd been online dating at the insistence of her cousin Bianca Beaumont Brown. And so far it had been more trouble than it was worth.

No one was serious, not really. Most of the men were simply window-shopping. Sedona popped another grape in her mouth as her latest prospect ran through her mind.

Tony Morton was a police officer for the city of Newport News, divorced and ready to settle down. He seemed like a nice person with a great personality, and after two weeks of talking on the phone they were finally going to meet.

So why aren't you excited?

He wasn't Webb. None of them were. She frowned and tossed the rest of the grapes into her mouth. She had told herself when she first agreed to start this journey it was time to let go. Derrick Webb — known — by everyone as simply Webb — would always be a part of her past. But after three years it was time to move on and fall in love again, or at least that's how her family felt. Everyone was concerned she wasn't dating. Her brothers were a different story all together. They wanted to see her happy, but even at her age, they still didn't like the idea of her being with any man.

Contrary to their thinking, just any man wouldn't do. She was looking for the right man. A hard truth indeed, and yet, she wasn't willing to settle for just anyone.

Sedona reached for a banana from a basket on the counter and sighed. She knew it was wrong, but she compared everyone to Webb. She couldn't help it. To have had someone who'd checked off almost every box on her list, it was hard to settle for less. And she refused. No matter how much Bianca scolded and called her picky, she just wasn't ready to simply settle. Webb had been her first and only love and she couldn't imagine being with someone just so she could say she had a man in her life.

I'd rather be alone.

But her cousins and her younger sister Sage weren't hearing it. In fact, she had been overruled. That's what happened when you came from a large family. And then there was her mother who called and checked on her constantly. The last thing she needed was to worry her even more.

As she leaned against the quartz countertop and chewed the banana, thoughts of Webb whirled in her brain. He had just returned from his first deployment when they had met. He was so charming with his wide smile and big brown eyes, she had fallen hard for him. Within two years they were engaged and had planned to marry after his second deployment.

Only he never came home.

They had been out in the Mediterranean Sea headed to an undisclosed location when a fire upon the ship had taken Webb's life, ripping out her heart.

Her chest contracted as she remembered the phone call from his mother. After that everything was a daze. Sedona barely remembered the events leading up to his funeral, while the day of his burial was a complete blur. After that it had taken her months to pull herself together. To help her cope, she started speaking at military installations about the selfless dedication of service members. She shared her story with thousands of others so they would know she truly understood. Over time, she had healed and decided it was time to move on because Webb would have wanted it that way. But that didn't make finding someone any easier.

While thinking about what she should wear, Sedona stepped into the sunroom location to the west of the house. Joggers were coming up the dock. The sun was starting to set on the water. She shifted her eyes to the Chesapeake Bay and from a distance she could see a cargo ship. There were also people out sailing in their private boats. The cloudless fall afternoon made the sky seem close enough for her to reach out and touch. She drew a long breath. The water always seemed to calm her nerves and had a way of making her feel at peace. While she stared, she decided to leave on what she was already wearing. The black pencil skirt, white chiffon ruffle blouse and red stilettos were perfect. Earlier, she had attended a women's empowerment luncheon at Norfolk State University and hadn't bothered to change.

Cocoa, her chocolate tabby, scurried into the room and started rubbing against her leg.

"What have you been doing all day?" she cooed as she reached down and gently stroked her across the body.

She loved her cat, but there was no denying it. She really was lonely for the type of affection only a man could provide.

Her stomach fluttered and felt like a million butterflies. She was suddenly looking forward to meeting Tony. Maybe, just maybe, her life was about to change.

◆ ◆ ◆

It was after eight when she returned home. Sedona lifted Cocoa into her arms and carried her up to her bedroom. Irritation rippled along her nerve endings. Within seconds her mind raced with conclusions. One in particular.

Maybe I'm meant to be single.

Because online dating just wasn't at all what she thought it would be. Tony had been nice, the conversation engaging, but once again there had been no chemistry.

She lowered Cocoa to the floor, then released the zipper and slid the skirt down over her hips. She was starting to wonder if she'd ever find it again. The sparks. Hands sweating. Her body heating with a single touch. Chemistry. That was what she was searching for and couldn't seem to find.

She removed her blouse and carried her clothes over to the wicker hamper in the corner and tossed them inside with a sigh of despair. Before she had even left the restaurant parking lot, Tony had sent her a text, letting her know he enjoyed their evening, and wanted to see her again. Too bad she hadn't felt the same way. A police officer would have been a nice addition to her rather large family. With five overly protective brothers, he wouldn't have been so easy to intimidate.

Sedona walked back over and took a seat on the bed then reached inside her purse for her phone.

She knew it was the cowardly way but there was no point in pretending.

Thank you for a lovely evening but I think we need to both continue our search.

Sedona hit Send and pushed her phone aside. It was the same message she had sent several times before. Some of the return responses had been far from nice, but she never believed in wasting time.

Maybe I'm just not meant to fall in love again.

The thought had filtered through her mind time and time again.

The evening proved her theory—you can't find

chemistry online. It was something you had to experience up close and personal.

Sedona dropped her head onto the yellow and white pillows decorating her bed and blew out another sigh flavored with disappointment. She was going to give online dating one more week. After that, she was deactivating her profile.

Chapter 2

Keith's eyes traveled over his crew. "Okay, listen up! There have been way too many safety violations," he announced then Keith went on to read the report he had received from safety. It was always the same old things: not wearing safety goggles, personnel caught without steel toe shoes. His crew was well aware anyone caught in unsecure areas without the proper security clearance was an automatic suspension from the naval shipyard.

"Today we're all working on the CIWS." The central intelligence weapon system was their bread and butter. "Pierce, you're gonna work with Tyler on the stern gate. Jasper, I want you with Mendoza working on the CIWS modification. The rest of you are working on the bow thrusters today. Any questions? No? Good, then get to work."

As his crew filed out the briefing room and headed toward the naval ship, he looked over at Bruce, the lead mechanic. "Make sure all of these projects are done correctly."

"I got this," he replied.

Bruce had been a shipfitter for years and was well aware how precise and important the proper measurements were. One mistake could upset the balance or the function of the aircraft carrier.

Keith gave him a curious look. "Are you getting out

of here for Thanksgiving?"

He nodded his bald head. "Yep. I don't feel like flying to my parents in Houston so I going to visit my grandmother at the nursing home. Maybe take her to Golden Corral. It's her favorite."

Keith thought about his own parents who had been divorced for over twenty years. His mother was taking a cruise for Thanksgiving, so this year he was planning to fly to Jacksonville and spend the holiday with his father and grandparents.

"While you're on leave, don't worry about this place. Abe's gonna fill in."

Keith met Bruce's hard stare and shook his head. The fifty-six-year-old was going through a divorce and would probably have bunked aboard the ship if the commander allowed it.

"He needs to be out tryna get laid," Bruce joked.

Keith laughed. "I agree he needs to find some way to blow off a little steam."

"That's an understatement."

They talked a few more minutes then Keith headed up toward the USS Harry S. Truman. Named after the thirty-third president, the ship was the size of a twenty-four story building and had seen lots of action in combat over the years. It was now at the shipyard for maintenance and upgrade. Keith felt pride tighten his chest knowing that as a shipfitter, he was instrumental in ensuring the ship was top notch before it set sail again.

While zipping up a heavy black hoodie, he walked up the bow to board the naval aircraft carrier. There were two checkpoints: one at the lower level, and the other at the top where military personnel checked for contrabands, cellular phones with cameras, and firearms.

"All clear, have a nice day."

Keith nodded. "You do the same."

He dropped by the stern gate, making sure repairs were underway, and assisted with a few calculations. By ten o'clock, Bruce had arrived to supervise the work. Never one to micromanage, Keith left the men to do what they were all paid to do, and headed down toward his office. If they needed him he had a company phone he carried at his hip.

Once he was off the ship and back in the building, Keith headed straight to the small office and stuck a pop tart in the microwave. He reached for his coffee mug and filled it with coffee he had brewed earlier that morning. Pop tart in hand, he walked over behind his cluttered desk and took a seat.

Keith reached for his phone, checked his emails and noticed he had a new message from BlackVAsingles.com, something that no longer excited him the way it used to. He clicked the icon, read the provocative message from Ms. Juicy and shook his head. Some women had no shame. Quickly, he deleted the message, but instead of closing the app, he decided to browse through his daily matches.

He wasn't sure why he even bothered. Most of the women he met online were only interested in the type of car he drove, and the size of his dick, instead of where his head and heart were. The only reason why he had even considered setting up a profile was because online dating was how his cousin had met his wife. Gloria was beautiful, talented and loved Brian as if there was no tomorrow. And no matter how much he tried to deny it, Keith envied the couple.

He clicked the link and scrolled through one potential candidate after the next, finding each one more disappointing than the last. *These are my matches?* He wondered, with a scowl. He was almost to the end when his eyes landed on a woman that caused his breathing to stall.

"No fucking way," he muttered.

His heart pounded wildly as he clicked the link to her photographs and then carefully he studied each, one by one. By the time he'd seen all eight photos, he knew for certain it was her.

Sedona Beaumont.

He knew those eyes anywhere, large, molten and mysterious. He used to lie in his bunk staring across at the wall where his bunk mate had posted his fiancée's photos with pride. Even now he couldn't take his eyes off the screen as he stared at her profile photo.

Sedona wore her hair shorter now, wild, wavy and surrounding her light brown face. In one of the photographs she wore an evening gown that hugged every delicious curve he'd had stored in his memory bank. In another, a pair of shorts skimmed the tops of her thighs, leaving endless long legs exposed. And then there was a corky smile with a slight overbite that was so innocent and sweet, it made a man want to hold her in his arms forever and never let go. That smile was what had been missing when he saw her that time at his friend's funeral. Keith's chest tightened as he remembered her cries, piercing the silent church while she stood at the altar.

At the cemetery it took everything he had to give his condolences and hand her the letter. He still remembered their encounter as if it had been just yesterday…

As he moved toward the gravesite, Sedona's head had been down but Keith had seen her face in photographs enough times, he had it committed to memory. Brown skin, long dark hair pulled up into a tight bun, exposing a slender neck.

"Excuse me...Sedona?"

Slowly she stared up at him and as their eyes locked he sucked in a long breath. She looked so distraught, yet beautiful.

She took his breath away.

Keith cleared his throat. "I'm Falcon, I served with Webb."

She inhaled, then let out her breath slowly while she blotted her cheek with the back of her hand. "Yes, yes of course," she managed between sniffles. "Thank you for coming."

Keith dipped his head in acknowledgement. "I'm so sorry for your loss. Webb was a great friend. He will definitely be missed."

She smiled at him – a sad smile. "Yes, he will," she replied in a soft, feminine voice.

He stood inches from her, his gaze measuring the undisguised pain in her dark eyes. Again, he cleared his throat. "I have something for you." Keith reached inside his pocket, removed the envelope, and unfolded it.

Her eyes widened. "What is it?"

"A letter... from Webb. He asked me to deliver this to you if anything ever happened."

Her right hand trembled noticeably as she reached for the envelope. Sedona then stared down at her name written in the familiar penmanship, and then clutched it tightly to her breasts.

"Donie, sweetheart. Are you okay?" A beautiful young woman said as she moved beside her. Sedona rested her head against the woman's thigh as her eyes filled with tears again.

"Thank you," she mouthed, then turned away and broke down with sobs again.

Desperate to separate himself from the sound piercing his heart, Keith nodded then rushed off to his car.

Keith pushed the memories aside and stared at the woman in the photographs. His favorite was a head shot of her with a pink backdrop. Sedona's arms were crossed. A saucy grin. A pair of glasses in her hand. Keith had a feeling she could persuade a man to do just about anything she set her mind to.

Seeking a committed relationship.

A smile curled his lips. He was glad to know that after three years she wasn't still mourning over her fiancé's death and had found the strength to get on with her life. Webb would have wanted it that way.

As he read and re-read her profile, Keith found his fingers itching to send her a message. But what would he say? "Hey, I'm Keith. I was the one who delivered Webb's letter at his funeral." No, despite the overwhelming desire to reach out to her he couldn't approach her. Attraction had its place and this wasn't it. Sedona once belonged to Webb. They had an unspoken rule not to date each other's exes, and he had to honor that no matter how hard it was to resist.

And he had a feeling it wasn't going to be easy.

Chapter 3

Sedona blew out a long breath and pushed away from the table. "I don't understand why planning a reunion is so hard!"

Laughing softly, Bianca Beaumont Brown rose from the barstool at the granite counter and padded across the wood floor to the refrigerator. "And you thought I was joking," she teased as she placed a glass under the automatic ice dispenser and pressed the button.

"I mean this is beyond ridiculous!"

Sheyna Simmons Beaumont, who was sitting to her right, gave a rude snort. "Now you see why I gave up on it."

Sedona combed her fingers through her hair and stared at the beautiful, mahogany woman with disbelief. Sheyna, married to her cousin Jace, had been trying for two years to plan a family reunion.

"Mom said you couldn't coordinate a date, but I really had no idea it was this hard to get those two to agree to anything."

Bianca was still laughing as she walked back over and leaned against the large center island. "Oh yeah, we've been pulling out our hair." She pointed to her short, trendy haircut that was perfect for her small oval-shaped face. The petite beauty didn't look old enough to have a six-year-old daughter.

Sheyna twirled around on the chair and gave Sedona a curious look. "Do you have any idea what the two of them have been feuding about all these years?"

Sedona's eyes traveled from one to the other before she shook her head. "I have no idea why my father and Uncle Roger won't speak to each other."

Bianca groaned, "Lord knows I've tried but Dad is so stubborn, and Mother says she can't even get him to talk about it to her."

She paused long enough to take a sip from her glass. "All I know is that it happened at a poker game. One minute the two were talking and laughing, and the next there was a shouting match and Daddy stormed out the door."

"Dammit! I wish I knew what it was about!" Bianca's walnut-colored eyes narrowed with frustration.

Sheyna nodded. "Me too. Jace has tried to find out but RB always changes the subject."

Sedona loved the way Sheyna called the founder of The Beaumont Corporation by a nickname. Apparently he was fond enough of her that it stuck, and he allowed the others to use it as well.

"Do you think they will ever reconcile?" Sheyna asked.

Bianca shrugged. "They are both so stubborn there's no telling, but I'm hoping this will be a way for mending bridges. Neither of them is getting any younger."

Sedona nodded. Her father had just turned sixty-five.

"So what are you going to do?"

Arms crossed against her small breasts, Bianca replied, "I say we just go ahead and plan the reunion and if they come they come, if they don't then they'll miss out."

Sedona gave a rude snort. "As stubborn as my father is, there's no way he's going to miss it."

"Mine either," Bianca added with a laugh.

Sheyna shook her head, sending her thick dark curls bouncing around her shoulders. "Well if that's the case, I could have had this thing organized a long time ago." The ladies shared a laugh, then discussed the itinerary for the reunion including a three-legged race across a private beach. By the time they had penciled in added costs, including airfare for a few of the distance relatives, Sedona breathed a deep sigh.

"Goodness, this is too much work!"

Sheyna agreed. "I know, right. My sister-in-law, Zanaa, is a wedding coordinator, and she loves doing stuff like this. I would lose my mind."

They went over the menu. Most of the meals were being provided by the Beaumont Hotel. The rest would be catered events at offsite locations.

"Summer in Sheraton Beach is going to be wild! Wait until the ladies get a look at your brothers," Sheyna teased.

Sedona playfully rolled her eyes as a smile turned her lips upward. "Thank goodness there are only three of them left. You have no idea what it was like growing up with five horny boys in the house."

Laughing, Bianca rose and walked over to a wine cooler next to the dishwasher and reached inside. "I got a pretty good idea," she began as she removed a bottle of red wine. "Remember I have three older brothers of my own."

Sheyna chimed in. "I only had two, but they were both a handful. Now that Darnell is engaged, my mother is no longer turning in her grave."

Bianca reached over for the wine cork. "I'm glad we got all that business out of the way. I'll get my assistant to start mailing out the invitations next week and see what kind of response we get."

Sedona laughed. "I'll make sure to have Mom put my dad's somewhere he can't miss it."

As Bianca grabbed three wine glasses from the cupboard and carried them over to the table, the garage door opened and a little girl raced in, followed by a tall handsome man.

"Hey sweetie," Bianca said and scooped her daughter close for a kiss. Sedona waved at London, then gazed adoringly at her little cousin. Sierra was beautiful with smooth brown skin like her mother and long, curly hair that she wore up in a ponytail.

"Donie!" she cried, then raced over and gave Sedona a big hug.

"Hey beautiful," she replied, then drew back and stared at her adorable face. Sierra's eyes were identical to Bianca's.

"Daddy took me to see Chuckie," she announced.

"Really?" Bianca turned to London and made eye contact. The look she gave was priceless. "More pizza, huh?"

Sierra nodded. "Yes, but Daddy had wings."

"Uh-huh... sounds like Daddy needs to stay away from the table," Bianca muttered and playfully patted his midsection.

Sedona giggled because London Brown was over six-feet and in excellent physical shape. He was also devilishly handsome. He usually wore a goatee, but now he was sporting a neatly trimmed beard. Dubbed the Chicken King, London was the owner of Clarence's Chicken & Fish House. The popular franchise had locations all around Delaware.

"Why are you hating on me?" London murmured as he leaned down and kissed his wife lovingly on the mouth.

I'm not hating, sweetheart. I'm just trying to watch your weight for both of our sakes. I need you around. Who else is going to take out the trash?"

"Ha-ha, your cousin here has jokes," he chuckled.

Sedona watched the way the two of them stared at each other as if no one was in the room but them. What she would give to have a man look that way at her.

They chatted for a while, and after London disappeared to his man-cave and Sierra went to her bedroom to play video games, the women moved to the family room and sprawled out across the leather furniture. Tomorrow they were going down on Main Street to shop before Sedona headed back to Hampton.

"So what's been going on with your social life?" she heard Bianca ask.

Sheyna chimed in. "Yeah, last time you were here you were dating someone who played basketball with Rance."

Sedona groaned and Bianca snickered knowingly.

Her brother Rance played for the Philadelphia 76ers, and she had made the mistake of dating the point guard, who turned out to be a self-centered prick.

Sedona had to laugh as she turned up her glass. "He was one mistake I will never repeat again."

"Have you been dating anyone else?" Bianca asked.

She wasted no time shaking her head. "Nope. No one worth mentioning."

The corner of Sheyna's eyes crinkled with curiosity. "But you're in Virginia. There are supposed to be lots of gorgeous men there."

"There are, but the good ones all seem to be taken." Sedona paused. "I don't want just anyone."

"Sedona, you're thirty-one. You need to hurry the hell up." Bianca's comment sent Sheyna in a fit of laughter.

"What I'm saying is, pick someone quick. How's the online dating going?" Bianca questioned.

"It's not," she replied between sips. "When I get home, I'm taking my profile down."

Sheyna's eyes shifted from one to the other. "Online dating? I heard if you're over thirty that's the best way to meet someone."

With a rude snort, Sedona replied, "I don't know where you heard that from, because all I've been meeting is rejects." While she sipped her wine, she went on to tell them about some of the dates she'd been having. Each tale sent her cousins screaming with laughter.

"He had on a Spanx?"

Sedona shot Sheyna a look. "Not only did he have it on, but he wanted to compare notes. Who does that?"

"Obviously, he does," Bianca teased.

"You have the App on your phone?" Sheyna asked with curiosity. Sedona nodded and she signaled for her to hand it over. "Let me see it."

Sedona reached insider her purse and retrieved her cell phone. "It's called Black Virginia Singles," she explained.

"Catchy name." Sheyna took the phone. Bianca slid over on the couch beside her to take a closer look, while Sedona returned to her chair. "Damn, there are some gorgeous men on here!"

"And I probably have already had a conversation with at least half of them. I don't know why Bianca has me wasting my time, "Sedona added with a scowl.

Bianca batted her lush lashes innocently. "What else do you have to do?"

"Ooh! There are also some scary looking creatures on this site," Sheyna said, laughing.

Sedona leaned back against the cushions feeling

totally uninterested. While the two browsed and joked, she allowed her mind to fill with thoughts of the upcoming holiday season. She was really hoping for a white Christmas this year, but in Hampton, the chances were slim.

"Oh look! Someone viewed your page?" Bianca cried.

Sheyna's brow bunched. "You can see who looked at her?"

"Uh-huh, click right there."

Sedona groaned and then muttered, "Who looked at my profile this time?" She could only imagine it was someone she wouldn't be the least bit interested in getting to know.

"Keeping it Simple...he's thirty-two, golden skin and...Daaayum, he's sexy! Come see!" Sheyna screamed.

Suddenly curious, Sedona rose from the chair and went to join the two. Sheyna slid over so she had room. Leaning close, she stared down at the screen and gasped. He really was gorgeous. There were six photos and each one more attractive than the last. Dimples. Dark wavy hair. Big brown eyes. And lips that looked delicious enough to suck.

"You should send him a message," Sheyna urged, breaking into her thoughts.

Sedona immediately shook her head. "Uh-uh, if he was interested he would have left me a message."

Bianca turned and looked at her. "Maybe he wants you to make the first move."

"Sometimes men can feel intimidated by a beautiful woman," Sheyna pointed out.

Sedona gave it a long thought. "I really don't think I have the energy to go out on another date."

"Please, Donie!" Bianca pleaded. "Just one last date, and if he's crazy then I'll deactivate your account for you."

"I'm with Bianca. He's too gorgeous to ignore. Message him and see what happens."

Sedona looked from one to the other and started laughing. "Hell, what do I have to lose?"

Bianca started clapping. "Yaay!"

"Okay, so what should I say?"

"I got this." Sheyna clicked on the message button. "I'm going to do just like he said, and keep it simple."

Sedona watched as Sheyna typed, **Hey Sexy**.

"*Hey Sexy*? Is that all you're going to say?" Bianca gawked.

Sheyna nodded. "Yep, and now all Sedona has to do is wait."

◆ ◆ ◆

"Touchdown!" George sprung from the chair. "Yeah boy!"

Keith groaned and stuffed another chip in his mouth. The Cowboys were down by four points with one quarter left. He'd been a diehard fan since he was eighteen, while his boy George Banks was all about the Steelers.

"It ain't over yet," he reminded him.

George chuckled loudly. "It might as well be. Cassel is getting his ass spanked."

"Shhh."

They turned and looked up to see George's pretty wife Adela stepping into the family room with a three-month-old boy cradled close in her arms.

"George, keep it down before you wake up Alan."

His whole demeanor changed. "Sorry babe." He sprung from the couch and walked over to kiss his wife tenderly on the lips.

Keith watched the two of them, wondering if he would ever find the same. Better yet, did he really want it? The wave of envy stirring at his gut said he did.

At the end of the first quarter, the Dallas Cowboys were up by seven and Keith's phone buzzed in his pocket. He dug it out and looked down at the screen and spotted another notification from BlackVASingles.com. Curiously, he pecked in his password and gazed down at the screen.

Hey Sexy.

He couldn't believe it. Sedona had messaged him.

Keith dragged a hand across his head then swung away from the television and stared down at the screen. Now what?

He should have known if he looked at her page, Sedona would know. *Way to go Falcon. Did she recognize me?* he wondered. Part of him hoped she had because it would have made an awkward situation so much easier. They could have met, he could confess who he was, and they could talk about Webb, and then go their separate ways. Only her flirty message hinted she had no idea who he was, which was probably a good thing, because his fingers had an altogether different plan.

You're the one who's sexy. What are you doing on a dating site?

He sat their frowning long after he'd hit Send. Flirting was not the right approach. But what was?

The truth.

The smart thing to do was to just come clean and tell her who he was, but he couldn't. Not yet. Not that he thought flirting was the way to go either.

"What are you doing?" George screamed at the

screen, pulling Keith's attention back to the football game.

He looked up just as Cassel tossed the ball thirty yards. "That's what I'm talking about!" Keith refocused his attention on the game and thoughts of Sedona were once again forgotten.

◆ ◆ ◆

Sedona checked into her suite at the Beaumont Hotel and was eager for a shower. After two glasses of wine too many, she was ready for an early night. Her cousins had plenty of room at their homes, but she preferred staying at the hotel.

The Beaumont Hotels were one of the most prestigious hotels in the country with locations dotting the map from coast-to-coast, with access to every amenity imaginable.

She wheeled a small rolling suitcase into the larger of the two bedrooms and opened it on the edge of the bed, then reached for the remote and turned on the television. She wasted no time climbing into the shower, then rumbling through her belongings until she found a conservative blue nightgown and wiggled it over her head. A chill skipped down her spine, and Sedona grabbed her iPad and slipped beneath the covers where it was nice and warm.

Tomorrow she was going to spend the afternoon with her cousin Jabarie, CEO of The Beaumont Corporation, and his wife Brenna. They had five gorgeous energetic children and the oldest, Bree, had a dance recital. Afterwards they were all going to Beaumont Manor to have dinner with her Aunt Jessica and Uncle Roger. Her cousins Jace and Jaden would be there as well with their families. They would have a great time catching up. Even though they lived within four hours of each other, with her busy schedule, Sedona was lucky to get to town a few times a year, so she was definitely looking forward to going to dinner tomorrow. Ever since Uncle Roger had decided to retire and turned over The Beaumont Corporation to his children, he seemed more relaxed and fun to be around. The last time she had seen him he had pulled her into a tight embrace. She went home and told her father, hoping the change would generate the urge for him to reach out to his older brother, instead he mumbled something under his breath and left the room.

She reached for her iPad, slid her finger across the screen and noticed she had a notification from BVS. What else was new? She checked her emails and responded to a few that required her attention before she finally decided to log onto BVS and see who she would have to block from contacting her. Sedona sighed. It was definitely the wrong way to think but with her past experiences, she didn't know how else to react.

She tapped the inbox icon with her finger, and her heart pounded when she realized she had a message from Keeping it Simple. By the time she'd finished reading it, Sedona was smiling from ear to ear.

She typed a quick response. **How are you?**

He must have been online because immediately he hit her back.

I'm good. How about you? BTW I'm Keith.

"Keith," she mumbled. It was definitely fitting. Curiously, she clicked onto his photographs. Now that her cousins weren't around, she had an opportunity to study his images without inquiring minds watching her every move. He was gorgeous, but there was something familiar about him. She just couldn't place it. He had the look of a bad boy, but he also looked like someone who would do anything to make sure she felt safe and protected.

The same way Webb had.

She typed a quick response.

Hi Keith, it's a pleasure to meet you. I'm Sedona. Why are you single?

He must have been online because immediately he responded,

How about I take you to lunch on Sunday and I tell you all about it? I would really like to meet you.

Sedona typed back, **I'd like that.**

Then let's not waste time. How about Panera Bread at one on Sunday?

Sedona was grinning while she typed, **It's a date.**

She then logged off the site and fell back on the bed with a grin. Maybe things were possibly looking up.

She could only hope.

Chapter 4

Sedona arrived back in Hampton late Saturday evening. She got up the next morning, walked across the garden to her office for a nine o'clock session with a client, and by eleven o'clock she was in her bedroom getting ready for her date with Keith.

As her eyes roamed over the clothes in her closet, she tried to decide what to wear. Part of her felt like going in the faded jeans and her favorite red sweater she was already wearing, because every time she went out of her way to look extra special she always ended up pissed for going to all that effort for nothing. But she was actually excited about the date and wanted to make a great first impression. It was crazy, because they hadn't spoken except for the online messages, including the one Keith sent this morning confirming lunch. Everyone else she had spent hours getting to know first.

And you see where that got you.

She had responded to Keith's message and given him her phone number just in case something changed. If he turned out to be a freak, she could always block his number.

Sedona finally settled on a pair of royal blue jeans, turquoise pumps and a matching V-neck sweater. She arrived at Panera's parking lot just as her cell phone rang. It was Keith.

"Sedona?"

The deep, husky sound of his voice caused her body to tremble with need. "Yes."

"This is Keith...I'm running just a few minutes late, but I'm on my way."

She had to struggle to find her voice. "Okay."

His voice was still vibrating in her ear as Sedona climbed out of her silver Jaguar and took a deep breath before shutting the car door. She had no idea why her heart was racing anxiously. It wasn't like this was the first time she had scheduled a meet and greet and knowing her luck it probably wouldn't be the last. But as she moved across the parking lot the anxiety continued. Sedona caught herself looking around as if Keith was possibly in the parking lot watching her. Goosebumps raced down her arm, and she even missed a step in her strut. *Get it together*, she scolded. She couldn't remember the last time a man had knocked her off her game. What was worse was they hadn't even met yet. Quickly, she hurried into the restaurant and took a deep breath before moving over to find a table. She decided on one close to the side door just in case she needed to make a hasty departure. As she slid onto the seat, Sedona realized she had a direct view to the front door. There was no way Keith could come inside either door without her noticing him first.

Reaching inside her purse, she retrieved her compact and stared down into the mirror at her reflection. She had taken a little extra time with her makeup. Not too much, but just enough to emphasize her large eyes and full lips. She put the compact away, then glanced around at the other customers either eating or chatting nonstop with each other. The fireplace was lit and several were sitting close by on the chairs.

Her eyes darted to the door as a man stepped inside.

She held her breath but released it when she realized it wasn't Keith. Although she had never seen anything but his photographs, she was certain she would know it was him the second she laid her eyes on him. Several more came through the door, and each time her heart sped up and then quickly slowed down.

"I am going to drive myself crazy," she muttered under her breath. Sedona decided to settle her mind and focused on Thursday. Thanksgiving was one of her favorites and it was a tradition they all spent the holiday at her parent's house. Her older brother Reese and his wife Dominique were flying in from Hawaii and would be staying in the area until the end of the year. Rance and his wife Debra would also be there with their new addition to the family, Tyrese Christopher Beaumont.

Sedona caught movement at the corner of her eyes and what she saw coming inside the restaurant made her draw a startled breath.

It was Keith.

Even though he was easy to identify, his photographs hadn't done him justice. He stepped inside oozing with confidence. Heads were turning and he seemed oblivious to the customers, who had stopped to stare with envy.

His wore dark jeans and a gray sweater that hung with perfection over his powerful build. With one sweep of his big brown eyes, he caused several women to swoon. They weren't the only ones. Sedona couldn't move. His handsome features and air of confidence incited panic. She refused to feel intimidated, but it wasn't easy.

Keith glanced around the restaurant and the moment he recognized her, his eyes sparked to life. Sedona drew in a long breath while his gaze drifted like a caress to her mouth, then lowered to her V-neck sweater.

She stood up and waited as he crossed the room to her. Heat came to life in her chest and then rose to her throat. When his attention came back to her face, there was no denying he liked what he saw. Good, because she felt the same way. The attraction was instant and she was unable to look away. Nervousness knotted her stomach, and buzzed between her thighs when he spoke in a voice like rich melting caramel.

"Sedona."

She nodded even though he wasn't asking a question.

"It's nice to finally meet you in person."

Clearing her throat, she replied, "Same here." She reached out her hand and the second he took it a hot sensation shot straight up her arms. She drew her hand back almost as if she had been burned and lowered back onto her seat. "Please sit," she said and realized her voice sounded hoarse. *Get it together.*

"Would you like something to eat?" he asked.

"I was thinking about maybe a salad."

"Then let's go order." Keith signaled for her to join him and she rose again. He placed a hand at the small of her back and she felt another rush of heat as they moved up to the front. *Talking about feeling lightheaded.* She could barely focus on the menu knowing he was just inches away and he smelled so amazing, she had to resist the urge to lean over and rest her head against his chest.

"Do you know what you want?"

It took a moment to realize Keith was talking about food and not him. "I think I'll have the chicken poppy seed salad and a green tea."

He winked. "Good choice."

She followed him to the register and listened while the baritone of his voice vibrated through her body. There was no way a man this fine could be single.

"That will be twenty-one, fifteen."

Sedona was reaching down for her wallet when she heard Keith say, "I got it."

She looked up and he winked again, then handed the cashier his debit card. In the past, she and her dates typically went Dutch on the meal. That way she didn't at all feel obligated to stay the entire meal, but with Keith, so far she was looking forward to spending time together.

They were back at their seats and not a moment too soon because her body was shaking so hard Sedona was afraid her knees would buckle at any second.

"What would you like to drink?" Keith was holding both of the empty cups in his hands. "Green tea, right?"

She nodded.

"A woman after my own heart," he murmured, his eyes seemed fixed on her lips making them tingle. "I'll be right back."

Sedona waited until he passed before she turned her head and stared after him. Gorgeous was an understatement. Keith was sexy as hell. She took a deep breath followed by another. It was crazy but she couldn't remember the last time a man made her body react so strongly.

Keep it together girl. You are acting like you've never met a handsome man before, when in fact she had. Only, it had been a long time since one made her body respond. In fact, she was so wrapped up in the attraction stirring between them, she had allowed a perfect stranger to get her drink.

"Here you go."

He returned carrying two green teas and placed one drink in front of her and another on his side of the table. *He could've dropped a roofie in your cup!* Now what? There was no way she was drinking that. Her father had taught her never to accept a drink from a stranger.

The buzzer went off before Keith even had a chance to sit down. "Let me go get our food," he said, and the second he turned his back, Sedona quickly switched the drinks and caught herself chuckling.

"Wait until I tell Bianca about this," she muttered.

"What's so funny?"

Startled, she looked up to see Keith was coming her way. "Nothing," she replied. "I saw something out the window that made me laugh."

He sat the tray down between them and took his seat. "They forgot to ask if you wanted a roll or an apple so I got one of each."

"I'll take the apple," she said and when he smiled, her body stirred again. Eating lunch with him wasn't going to be easy. Sedona decided if she focused on her lunch instead of the dessert sitting across from her, maybe she'd get her body to behave.

"So tell me something about you. You from Hampton?"

Sedona shook her head. "No, I'm from Richmond. I moved here after college."

"Where'd you go?"

"William and Mary." She took a sip. "What about you?"

"I'm originally from Jacksonville but my father was in the Navy so I lived all over the place," he managed between chews. Her gaze shifted down to watch his lips as they moved. Goodness, they looked so delicious, she could almost taste them.

Clearing her throat, she snapped out of it. "What kind of work do you do?"

He shifted on the chair in a relaxed stance and she felt

heat warming her midsection. "I'm working as a supervisor at the Portsmouth shipyard."

Sedona stuffed her mouth and listened as he talked about working as a shipfitter on one of the naval ships. "Sounds interesting," she said. A blue collar worker. She found them so sexy.

"I'm a motivational speaker and a life coach."

Keith cocked one eyebrow the way Dwayne Johnson did in the movies and Sedona found herself licking her lips. "Please tell me more."

"What do you want to know?" she purred and realized she was flirting.

"Well, you can start by telling me what a life coach does." He bit into his sandwich and waited for her to continue.

She took a sip of her tea and said, "Clients hire me to help them set and achieve goals. My job is to help them succeed."

He looked amused. "What do they do? Come to your office and sit on your couch, like at a shrink's office?"

She laughed. "Nope. Most of my clients never meet me in person. I counsel them forty-five minutes a week over the phone."

"You're kidding?"

Sedona shook her head and smiled. "No not at all. I motivate individuals and help them to achieve a better balance in their lives. I do webinars and speaking engagements, as well," she said and paused to wipe her mouth with a napkin. "Tomorrow I speak at a women's liberal conference at Old Dominion University."

He genuinely looked impressed.

"I work with a concept called *forward thinking*, and have been empowering people, mostly women for years."

"Interesting. I've never met a life coach before."

"And I've never met a shipbuilder." She caught him smiling at her. "What?"

Keith leaned forward. "I gotta know… why a beautiful woman is on a dating site?"

And he was too fine for words. Sedona was having a hard time staying focused.

As she mixed the dressing on her salad a blush warmed her cheeks. "I could say the same about you."

He smirked then said, "You haven't answered my question."

"Actually my cousin set up my profile." Sedona stopped to grin. She could already hear the conversation the two of them would be having later. "I haven't dated in a while. I don't do nightclubs. I work from home, so how else was I going to ever meet anyone?" she concluded and speared a piece of chicken with her fork. "What about you? You don't look anything at all like the men I've been meeting online."

Leaning in slightly, he asked in a low voice, "And what kind is that?"

Was he flirting with her? Sedona's breath hitched, and she had to swallow before speaking. "Nothing like what they've written on their profile."

Keith tossed his head back and the laughter vibrated through her body again. "I've had a couple of those."

She was intrigued. "Really? Women play the same games?"

"Hell yeah. I've had one who'd been using her younger sister's picture, who happened to be two-hundred pounds lighter."

Sedona giggled as she chewed. "Oh my! What did you do?"

"I figured she must have been after a free meal so I

fed her," Keith said and then continued his story.

Within minutes, she was practically in tears.

"That chick had the nerve to order a T-bone steak."

"What?" she gasped.

As he bit into a chip, he said, "And dessert." His eyes danced with amusement and she noticed the dimples at both cheeks. "After dinner was over, I walked her to her car and wished her luck."

As a psychologist, Sedona was seeing a classic case of low self-esteem. "Did she ever call you again?"

"Luckily we'd never exchanged numbers. When she hit me up on the site, I told her there wasn't any connection. She cussed me out for getting her emotionally involved."

"You should have cussed her out for ordering a T-bone." Sedona gave another throaty laugh as Keith drew to the conclusion of his story. "I guess you must have that kind of effect on women."

"I don't know how. All I did was feed the chick."

"For some that's enough."

Keith shrugged and bit into his sandwich. "What about you? I'm sure you've broken a heart or two in your lifetime."

No, I was the one with the broken heart. "No, not really. I've met several creeps and a few nice guys but no one worth calling home to tell Daddy about."

Keith reached for his drink and took a sip. "Oh, so they had to pass the Daddy test?"

She nodded and brought the fork to her lips. "Absolutely. He's gotta be good enough to take home to meet my father and brothers."

Keith took a sip from the straw while he studied her. "How many brothers do you have?"

"Five and they are ridiculously overprotective of me

and my sister Sage. Although my sister can hold her own."

"How so?"

Sedona chewed on a dinner roll as she pulled her words together. "I love my sister, but she is an alpha and very dominant. My brothers say no man in his right mind is going to stick around for too long." She paused and they shared a laugh. "Sage has an engineering degree but prefers working as an auto mechanic. We call her Dr. Fix-It."

"Really?" His expression was incredulous.

Sedona nodded. "My father owns a dealership and out of the seven of us, the only ones interested in taking over someday are my brother Rush and Sage."

"Which dealership, if you don't mind me asking?" Keith asked between chews.

She wasn't sure why she was rattling off all her personal business to a total stranger, but there was something about Keith that made her feel at ease. "Beaumont Automotive Group."

His eyes widened. "You're a *Beaumont*?"

Dammit, she had given him her last name. Something she'd rarely ever done until she had a chance to really get to know the guy and ensure he wasn't a creep. Sedona nodded. "Yes, that would be me."

As he chewed, she could see the wheels turning in his head. "I remembered reading Beaumont Automotive Group is related to the same family that owns the Beaumont Hotels."

She nodded. "Yes, that's my uncle."

Keith shook his head. "Wow! I'm sitting across the table from royalty."

Sedona gave him a dismissive wave. "Whatever. We're just regular folk." The look he gave said he didn't agree with that analogy. "Tell me about you," she asked suddenly feeling uncomfortable about being in the spotlight and went back to eating her salad.

"Well I'm Keith Falcon of the Jamestown Falcons, a small city right outside of Jacksonville."

"Is that a professional football team?"

He was laughing at her again. "No, that's the Jaguars. My father is the mayor of Jamestown."

"Seriously?"

He nodded. "He's been the mayor for almost fifteen years, because no one wants to run against him."

"That sounds like that's a good thing."

"Yes, but in a town with a population of three thousand that isn't saying a whole lot." He winked.

It was her turn to laugh. "What does your mother do?"

"My mother is a seamstress, owns a small dress shop in Charlottesville. Sewing is all she's ever really enjoyed doing."

She finished chewing and asked, "And do you have any brothers or sisters?"

"A younger brother. Xavier is in the Air Force. He joined right after I got out of the Navy."

Her eyes widened. "You were in the Navy? How long were you in?"

He reached for his soda and took a long swallow before speaking. "Twelve years before I was medically discharged for an ankle injury." He searched her face. "Do you have something against the military?"

Sedona swallowed the lump in her throat. "No, I have a lot of respect for the military."

He smiled and seemed relieved by her answer. "Tell me Sedona…what are you looking for in a relationship?"

"Hmm…I   guess   what   everyone   wants.

Chemistry...compatibility," she replied and stabbed the last slice of chicken.

"And how has that worked out for you so far?"

She frowned. "I've had it once and hope to someday find it again." She took another bite. "What about you?"

Keith shook his head. "I spent too many years running from commitment."

"Really? Please elaborate."

He finished chewing a potato chip and took a sip before answering, "I don't know what it was, but for years relationships scared me."

"And now?"

Leaning forward, Keith licked his lips and replied, "Now, I'm at a different place in my life and I look forward to meeting that special someone."

The action was so damn sexy it was all she could do to keep it together.

◆ ◆ ◆

While his gaze was held captive by her piercing sable-colored eyes, Keith decided to take the opportunity to study Sedona's beautiful features. Her rich, brown hair was thick and curling around a round face. She had those come-and-get-me eyes and full pink lips that curved in a perfect bow that made a man want to slip his tongue inside and taste them all night long. He couldn't remember the last time his body — one part in particular — leapt to attention after a single sultry look.

Holy shit.

He was attracted to her. He was drawn to her in a way he was too weak to ignore. So much for holding his hunger in check and revealing his true identity. Right now all he saw was a gorgeous woman sitting across the table, giving hints that she was equally attracted to him. "You're beautiful."

"Thank you," she replied and he loved the way she dropped her eyes and blushed.

"What nationality are you?" he asked.

"I'm African-American and Samoan," Sedona replied as she took a sip from her straw.

Their eyes locked and Keith felt a tug at his chest. "The combination is incredible," he said and searched her face. "Now I'm curious to know if you like what you see."

Sedona's eyes widened. "Wow, you don't hold back, do you?"

He shrugged and was pleased to see at least she was still smiling. "Why waste time? I believe in finding out right off the bat if the attraction is mutual."

"It's definitely mutual. I find you quite sexy," she purred and then a saucy grin curled her lips. "Although, a woman will say just about anything until she's safely back in her car. That way she doesn't have to see your face when she ends it."

"Is that so?" he said as if he didn't already know.

"Uh-huh." She nodded her head. "She'll get in her car and send you a nice, "It's not you, it's me" message and that will be the end of that."

"Is that what you're planning on doing?"

"I guess you'll soon find out." Grinning, she rose and carried her tray over to the trash, leaving him sitting there by himself.

There was no way Keith was letting her get away.

Quickly, he rose and dumped his trash, then walked out the restaurant and fell into step beside her.

Tilting her head, Sedona smiled up at him and said, "Thank you for lunch."

Keith playfully shook his head. "This date isn't over until I walk you safely to your car." He saw the way her eyes widened as he placed a hand at her waist and led her toward the parking lot. The contact had his loins tightening with the need to possess her.

"I see you have a slight limp. Is that the ankle injury you were talking about?" Sedona studied him, her eyes twinkling with genuine concern.

"Yeah, somedays you can barely tell, and other days it's noticeable. But it's nothing a little ibuprofen can't cure." He smiled down at her.

Once she reached a sleek, gray Jaguar, she stopped and turned to him. "Okay, so let's try this again...thank you for lunch."

Keith swept a hand up to cup her cheek, his fingertips tracing lightly along the lines of her jaw. "The pleasure's all mine."

She had the sweetest looking lips. Kissable. For all the reasons he tried to convince himself it would be a mistake, he couldn't help but wonder what it would feel like to kiss her.

So he crushed her to him.

And desire stirred.

♦ ♦ ♦

For the first time in over three years, Sedona Beaumont craved passion, and she knew exactly who she wanted it from.

Keith.

She tilted her chin upward and his lips captured hers. Instantly, an inferno ignited between them that was so explosive it almost dropped her to her knees. Need and passion. That's all she could think about. She wanted nothing more than to feel everything Keith had to offer, and she desired everything he was willing to give.

Keith growled against her lips and the sound was so primitive and arousing, it intensified her need. His lips were hot. Wet. Succulent, and so sinfully delicious.

He brought his arms around to her back and she brought her hands up to cup his waist. Parting her lips, his tongue slid inside and he deepened the kiss. Desire reverberated through her body before settling hot and heavy between her thighs.

The kiss went on and on until Sedona finally ended the kiss. She took a moment to catch her breath, then slowly opened her eyes to find him staring down at her.

"I may have gotten a little carried away," Keith confessed with a simple smile that placed dimples at both of his cheeks.

Maybe. Maybe not. "I'm not complaining," Sedona admitted and her tongue slipped out from between her lips. Dammit, she was flirting again.

"Good," he replied and raised his hand to gently caress her cheek. "Because I'm not apologizing."

"And I would have been mad if you had," she decided with a smirk.

"How about we go out again before the holiday?"

His request caused her pulse to race. "I'd like that."

"Excellent. I'll call you." Keith leaned in preparing to kiss her, but jerked back. "That's if you really wanna see a brotha again and not just saying that until you're safely in your car?"

Sedona was so tickled she started laughing. He joined in, and then kissed her soundly on the mouth. The kiss was brief, but no less powerful than the last.

"You don't have to answer. Call and let me know."

With a nod, Sedona chirped the locks and opened the door but before climbing in, she paused to gaze up at him again. "It was nice to finally meet you Keith."

He winked. "The pleasure was mine."

♦ ♦ ♦

Sedona pulled away from Coliseum Drive. She was shaking and smiling so hard, she was surprised she didn't run into the car in front of her because she totally zoned out.

No way. How was it even possible? Their time together had been an hour tops, and yet she was already hungry for so much more.

A trembling smile curled her lips. She hadn't felt this alive in years. Even when she'd decided to start dating again, no one—not any of the guys she had met—had made her feel as if she was floating until now.

Heat rushed to her chest and caused her nipples to bead with desire as she remembered the way Keith licked his lips.

He was so sexy!

Finally, after all this time, she had met a man that made her think there was a chance at falling in love again. And it felt really good. She released another long shaky breath.

By the time she pulled on to her street and gazed out onto the Chesapeake Bay, she was truly starting to believe her personal life was starting to look up for her.

Her professional life had never been a problem. She'd graduated at the top of her class and went on to excel at everything she had done and when she made the decision to step away from a six-figure position and focus on life coaching, she never looked back. Her grandfather, Roger Beaumont I, had left all of his grandchildren enough money to live comfortably for the rest of their lives, so it wasn't about the money. It was about doing something that made a difference.

Sedona walked into the house and immediately kicked off her heels. She loved the way her legs looked in pumps, but they were killer on her calves. As she was moving through her formal living room, she spotted something on the mantel that made her stop and draw a deep breath — a picture of her and Webb when they were dreaming about an exciting life ahead.

As she reached for it a lump clogged her throat. She thought she'd never get to the point when she would feel excited over someone other than Webb, and yet today she had. Did that mean she had finally closed that chapter in her life?

"Webb, I'll never forget you," Sedona whispered, while she traced her fingers along his face. She had a feeling he was smiling down from heaven at her.

After returning the photo to the shelf, she moved down the hall, and climbed the stairs with tears in her eyes and a smile on her lips.

Yep, things were definitely looking up.

◆ ◆ ◆

Webb was probably turning in his grave.

After Sedona left, Keith walked over to *Sports Authority* to buy another pair of goggles. He loved to swim every chance he got and planned to start back after the holidays. He left the store, then made it out to his BMW 645Ci, climbed in, and put the key in the ignition. Only he didn't bother to pull off. Instead, he blew out a long unsteady breath.

Sedona Beaumont fascinated him. Every muscle in his body had recognized her beauty. He ached to taste her slender throat, among other things. Even now thoughts of her excited him. Part of him felt guilty, while the rest of him enjoyed being around her so much, there was no way he could ignore the mental and physical connection.

When they had agreed to meet for lunch, he'd had no idea how beautiful she was. Sure, he'd seen the photographs and she had been beautiful, even when she was grieving, but today her beauty had caught him off guard. Her features were breathtaking, Keith concluded, as he put the car into gear and pulled off.

The entire time he was kissing Sedona, his hands ached to skim her slender legs and to feel her round ass. All the while they ate, her scent tightened every muscle in his body. But what shook him most was the instant need to stake his claim on her. A woman he had known as Webb's fiancée and yet even despite the guilt, he wanted her in his bed. As he jumped onto the highway and drove from zero to eighty in lightning speed toward his townhouse, he thought about making love to her; slow, sensual love, all night and into the morning; and sliding deep inside her body, again and again. His loins tightened painful at the mere thought.

Dammit, he scowled. Why her? Of all the women in Virginia, why Webb's girl? Maybe it was those thick, lush lashes that practically brushed her high cheekbones, or the depths of her sable-brown eyes that had him imagining things he had no business thinking.

Whatever it was, it was enough to let him know he had to have her.

As he pulled off the highway, Keith mulled over every second of their encounter. He'd had numerous opportunities to be honest and tell her who he was, only he hadn't.

Why is that?

Because deep down he knew if Sedona had known who he was, he would have lost any chance of getting to know her intimately. Selfishly, he couldn't risk that. He wanted her and dammit, he was going to have her.

Chapter 5

It took two days before Sedona contacted Keith, and it wasn't because he wasn't on her mind, it took that long because she didn't want to appear desperate.

It was stupid the games people played, but dating wasn't something she had ever been good at, which was part of the reason why it had taken her so long to get back out on the scene.

While she brushed her hair, she stared at her reflection in the mirror and thought about what she was feeling. Ever since they'd met for lunch she hadn't been able to stop thinking about Keith. The magnetic smile, golden brown skin, the precision haircut and a thin mustache over a pair of sensuous lips, the images she couldn't get out of her mind. And then there was that voice dreams were made of. She'd heard it in her sleep at night, and when she had spoken to him over the phone the sound had her toes curling in her boots.

Keith had a way of making her feel she'd been waiting all this time for him to walk into her life.

She cleared her throat and frowned. *Slow it down, Sedona.* The last thing she wanted was to get ahead of herself and make more of what was going on than there really was. It would only be their second date so only time would tell where the relationship went from there. However, the only thing she knew for certain was that she was very attracted to Keith.

At six o'clock, Sedona took one final look in the full-length mirror. She had spent the afternoon shopping for something that complemented her curves. The skinny designer jeans she was wearing fit her hips like a glove and were worth the hefty price tag. She had paired them with a soft orange cashmere sweater that made her breasts look amazing.

While turning from side to side, she gazed down at the brown leather boots she had found at a country and western store. She had never thought of herself wearing cowboy boots, but they were a perfect tie-in to her outfit.

She glanced again at the reflection of her oval face, framed by wisps of curling hair, then reached for her favorite Calvin Klein perfume and dabbed a little behind her ears and at her wrists, then smiled softly. *If you look good you need to smell good as well.* That was her motto.

The doorbell chimed, sending her pulse racing. Sedona looked over at the clock on her nightstand and mumbled, "A man who knows how to be on time."

Quickly, she fingered her curls then headed down the stairs. As soon as she reached the door, Sedona drew in another breath—an ill attempt at calming her nerves— then turned the knob and opened it.

"Hi," she said and it took everything she had not to purr with pleasure as Keith stepped inside. Their eyes locked and she felt an unmistakable pull toward him.

"Hello Sedona." He leaned forward and pressed his warm, wet lips to hers. "You look beautiful," Keith commented as he drew back. He was watching her closely, and there was no way she could ignore the desire kindling in the depths of his eyes. Sedona forced herself to take a deep breath.

"Thank you."

Dammit, he was so freaking sexy! There were the black jeans that relaxed on his hips and left plenty of room for whatever he might be packing between his thighs and she had a sneaky feeling he was packing plenty. He was wearing a Dallas Cowboys hoodie and white sneakers were on his feet.

"Let me grab my jacket." She turned and did her best not to stumble as she made the short distance over to the coat closet. He looked and smelled so good that she wasn't sure how she was going to get through the rest of the evening.

Once they were in his car and Keith pulled down the street, Sedona felt her body starting to relax.

"Are you going to tell me where we're going?"

He took his eyes from the road and gave her a mischievous smile. "Nope, but I hope you like pizza and hot wings."

Laughing, she nodded. "Yes, I do."

Keith winked. "Good, then we should have a good time."

Grinning, she leaned back and got comfortable on the seat. He had given her instructions to dress comfortably but that's where the information had ended.

Keith looked over at her and Sedona felt her insides coming to life again. "How's the motivational speaking world?"

"Great, I've landed an interview with Laila Ali."

"No shit?" he looked clearly impressed.

She licked her lips and tried to collect her thoughts. It wasn't easy with Keith sitting there looking so attractive. "Yes, as part of my Living Your Success series." She went on to tell him about the new book she was writing. Her editor had assisted her in scheduling interviews with several random celebrities in different areas of entertainment.

"That's amazing. You're doing the damn thang."

Sedona laughed. "Thank you. How's the shipyard?"

"We just landed another large contract so that means my crew can breathe easy during the holidays because they'll have a job to return to."

"Is the shipyard exclusively government contracts?"

With a nod, Keith replied, "The naval shipyard belongs to the Navy. We specialize in repairing, overhauling and modernizing ships and submarines. Right now we're making some upgrades to the USS Harry S. Truman."

"Sounds interesting. Do you like what you do?"

"It has its moments," he muttered. "But nothing will ever beat life as sailor traveling overseas." Before she could question him further about being in the Navy, Keith pulled his vehicle into a parking lot.

Sedona looked out the windshield and spotted the flashing neon sign overhead, and immediately her head whipped around. "You're kidding, right?"

His gaze didn't even flicker. "It will be fun."

They were parked in front of Skate King.

"Have you ever been skating before?" he asked and killed the engine.

While staring at the roller rink, Sedona laughed. "Yes, as a kid."

Keith flashed a rueful grinned then reached over and touched her arm. "Well, then get ready to feel like a kid again."

He opened the door and climbed out and she sat there amused, wondering if he was truly serious.

When he came around and opened the door, Sedona stared up at the laughter tickling his lips. "Are we really going in there?"

With a nod he wrapped his long fingers around her upper arm lifting her up from the seat and onto her feet.

"That's why I said dress comfortably." Music was flooding from inside the building out into the parking lot. Her heart fluttered with excitement.

"Okay, but if I fall on my face don't say anything," she said and pointed her finger at him.

Keith took a hold of her hand and dragged her close. Gazes locked, he whispered, "The good thing is if you do, I'll be there to catch you."

He, then, kissed her. It was nothing like their first kiss. It was far better.

◆ ◆ ◆

The first taste of her lips turned Keith's stomach inside out. He'd expected heat and evidence of the hunger that had been building over the past few days. What he hadn't expected was the overwhelming need to possess her. Whoa! The impact blew his mind and made him want to devour her.

Keith pulled her tightly to him, loving the way her curves felt beneath his fingers. With a moan, Sedona brought her arms up around his neck. That was all the encouragement he needed. He parted her lips with his tongue, and slipped inside. The first taste of her staggered him until he was forced to lean her back against his car. How the hell could one kiss have such a powerful impact? Better yet, how in the world had she managed to make him feel so out of control? No woman had ever made him feel like this before. Never. Not that he was complaining.

Sedona's mouth was becoming an addiction. She had awakened a need in him that he hadn't been unaware of and now that he'd tasted her, held her lush body in his arms, Keith knew kissing her would never be enough. He wanted to draw her legs up, wrap them around his waist, and bury his cock deeply within her.

Whoa!

Even as the thought infiltrated his mind, he fought for control. He needed to take things slow. They still needed to talk before he could take what was developing between them to the next level.

Sedona moaned, and the soft breathy sound snapped through his thoughts and then traveled downward, warming his blood at every corner. He continued to kiss her while trying to wrap his brain around what was happening. The last thing he needed was to move too fast. Yet, he knew for certain was it no longer mattered that she had once belonged to Webb. All he knew was he wanted her in his life.

It took a great deal of willpower to draw away from the kiss, drop his forehead against hers and just breathe his way back to sanity. It was probably one of the hardest things he had to do — draw back, and wait for the lust to fade.

Lifting his head, he stared at Sedona, her eyes were sparkling, and he resisted the urge to draw her close and ravish her mouth again.

Sedona blew out a breath then slid away from him. "Wow!" she whispered between breaths as she raised her hands to thread them through her hair.

"You can say that again." He reached out and stroked her cheek. She was so pretty. Big eyes, soft skin, and lips that fit perfectly along his. "Now that we've gotten that out the way, let's go have some fun," he forced himself to say. Although he knew after one taste skating was far from his mind. Instead, he'd rather stand in the parking lot and pass the time kissing Sedona. His insides burned and staring down at her moist lips was only stoking the flames. The only way to keep the need burning at his chest in check was to keep the conversation going and keep his hands to himself.

◆ ◆ ◆

Sedona could barely catch her breath under the impact of his kiss. Keith was pure temptation, she told herself. One who was going to be hard to resist. She liked being close to him, even though she couldn't think straight when she was.

"You ready to go in?" he asked.

The sun was long gone, but overhead lighting bathed the parking lot. She smiled and congratulated herself for not stammering like an idiot.

"Lead the way, Romeo."

Sedona couldn't remember the last time she'd had so much fun.

Keith had failed to mention it was couple's night at the rink and everyone was skating in pairs. Just like she thought, Sedona fell, but Keith was a man of his word and immediately scooped her up off the floor, and held her hand again. The moment their fingers touched, her body snapped, crackled and popped so much Sedona was sure that was the reason she had fallen the first time. When he brought his hand to her waist, her heart galloped in excitement. As a result, she had a hard time finding her rhythm. Keith, on the other hand, had no trouble. He moved with such skill Sedona felt proud to be his partner. He knew all the skate moves, including how to properly stop. It was as if his feet never came off the ground. Whatever it was, he definitely looked sexy doing it.

The rink was like a seventies dance club where all of the couples were dancing in their skates, caught up in the disco fever. There were strobe lights overhead and smoke. Seventies recording sounds. Some people were wearing bell-bottoms and disco pants like John Travolta wore in the classic movie, *Saturday Night Live*, and large afros.

The Bee Gees were singing, "Staying Alive," and when Donna Summers started singing, "Hot Stuff", Sedona couldn't sit still even if she had wanted. She danced stiffly beside Keith making sure she didn't fall, but when "Bounce, Rock, Skate, Roll" came on, Keith took her hand and she danced beside him staying in rhythm. The experience brought back so many memories of her childhood and being dropped off at the rink with her skates hanging by the shoe laces draped over her shoulder.

After a few sets they were sitting on a bench, sharing an order of nachos with jalapenos.

"How'd you learn to skate so well?" she asked while licking cheese from her fingers.

Keith stretched his long legs out in front of him as he spoke. "I used to spend all my summers at the skating rink. That was the best way to pick up chicks."

"What?" she cried and when he wagged his brow, she started laughing.

He shrugged innocently. "Hey I was a teenager with raging hormones. My grandfather made us work at the cleaners to earn money."

"Your grandfather owns a dry cleaners?"

"He owned a chain of cleaners. Ten to be exact."

"Wow!" She stopped and paused for a thoughtful moment. "So if I needed you to come over and press my suit, would you object?"

"I don't think I could say no to you." He stroked his tongue along his lips and conjured erotic thoughts.

"Why is that?" she said and realized she was flirting again.

"Babe, you are simply irresistible."

Sedona laughed. He sure was a charmer.

The next question she asked was an attempt to keep her head on straight.

"So I guess this is where you take all your first dates?" She twirled her finger, indicating the music, and couples skating.

"Only the special dates," Keith said and then winked.

"I'm special? Wow! I'm flattered." She teased while looking at his lips.

His mouth curved into a wickedly sexy smile. "The second you stepped out of your house and I saw all *that* in them jeans, your ranking soared on my chart." He wagged his brow again.

She laughed along with him.

"No seriously, I've only brought one other woman here and we weren't skating five minutes when she fell on her ass and then she insisted I take her home." Keith looked around the rink, expression blank. "I like a woman with a sense of humor. Life is too short to be serious all the time."

Sedona smiled and rocked her feet to the tune of, "Let it Whip". "I can't argue with you there," she said while thinking of one of her online dates who'd barely cracked a smile all through dinner. "My elementary teacher used to say the same thing and it stuck with me through high school and college."

They finished the nachos followed by a pound of hot wings. They'd managed to talk for almost the entire time and it felt good to swap childhood stories.

They had grown up on opposite sides of the street and yet there was a lot they had in common, but also enough of a difference to make what they had brewing between them even more exciting. As Sedona gazed up into his gorgeous eyes that sparkled with life each and every time he spoke about something obnoxious he and his brother had done growing up, she realized she wanted much more with Keith Falcon than just a few simple dates.

The music had slowed down and he tilted his head, then rose from the bench with one push. "Come on." They were about to get all close and personal and her heart pounded beneath her breasts with anticipation. Keith reached down for Sedona's hand and she rose. Her eyes scanned the dance floor where couples were skating, arms wrapped around each other, hips gyrating as if they were slow dancing.

Keith steered Sedona out onto the floor, then moved behind her and placed his hands at her waist. "This time we're gonna skate backwards."

"What...backwards?" She tried to swing around, but he held her firmly in place.

"Relax, you're gonna do fine. Didn't they teach you how to ice skate backwards?" His breath curled about her neck, kicking her pulse into overdrive.

She swallowed and looked nervously down at the floor. "Well...yeah."

"Same concept. Just imagine you're ice skating and follow my lead."

Only she didn't feel his level of confidence, especially since the heat of his body close to hers was enough to throw her off her game. Her body tightened and her blood roared.

"Just remember you're not walking backwards.

Position your feet with toes inward and knees slightly bent. Now we're gonna start out slow," he whispered close to her ear and then he was pulling her along with him. Sedona gasped and struggled to match his pace.

"Relax and let me lead," he whispered.

She drew a deep breath.

"That's it. Glide and lift. Glide and lift."

Sedona couldn't believe it. They were skating close, side by side, moving at a slightly faster pace. The arm he brought around to cup her waist she leaned back into it slightly and allowed the music and comfort of his body to lead her. Rick James's "Fire and Desire" was blaring from the speakers, and she allowed her body to relax and feel the music. Skating with Keith was practically the most romantic dance she had ever done. He was right. It was a lot like ice skating, only better. Turning her head, Sedona looked up at Keith and saw desire burning in his gaze. She was relieved to see she wasn't the only one caught up under the sensual spell.

They skated two sets then the music changed and there was a long conga line to the "Double Dutch Bus" followed by "Boogie Oogie Oogie". By nine they wrapped up the evening with Taana Gardner's, "Heartbeat". Sedona had a feeling she could have stayed until the stating rink closed at eleven, but decided it was time to call it a night or she'd never get up. She had a conference call scheduled for seven o'clock in the morning.

"What time is your flight to Jacksonville on Thursday?" she asked, on the drive back to her house.

"Eleven o'clock. We eat late on Thanksgiving." He was spending the holiday at his grandparent's house. Last night while on the phone, he had explained that his parents had been divorced since he was in middle school, and each year Keith alternated where he spent the holiday.

By the time they'd made it to her house, Sedona realized she wasn't in any rush for Keith to leave. "I have a fire pit out back. You want to come around and join me?"

◆ ◆ ◆

If Keith had any sense left, he would have declined and simply walked Sedona to the door, but he was hard-headed, especially when it was something he really wanted.

And that something was Sedona Beaumont.

Every second he spent with her just reiterated what he already knew. He couldn't just walk away. Not when everything between them felt so right.

The conversation. The chemistry. The kisses they had shared. He craved everything Sedona and he couldn't have resisted her now even if he wanted, and he didn't.

"Sure, why not?"

Their eyes connected and then she grinned and headed to the massive ornately- carved mahogany doors. He followed the sway of her lush hips up the stairs, loving the way she strutted confidently in her boots.

Keith went inside and spotted something furry moving down the hall.

"You have a cat."

Sedona tossed her keys into a bowl on the hall table and smiled over her shoulder. "Yes, that's Cocoa. Are you afraid of cats?"

He shook his head. "Nope. My mom has a white Persian named Snowball."

"Cocoa is old and set in her ways. Most the times I

forget she's even here," she explained as he followed her down a long foyer, with twelve-foot cathedral ceilings, to a grand sunroom that had breathtaking views of the Chesapeake Bay and the lush property surrounding her home.

"You have a stunning waterfront property."

"Thank you. I happened to stumble upon it by accident," Sedona explained as she stepped out the sliding door.

"I met the previous owner walking out to the mailbox. I asked her for directions to a seafood restaurant not too far from here. She gave me directions, but not before we struck up a conversation about this beautiful neighborhood. And I found out she was putting the house on the market."

Keith noticed there were lights along the deck floor and posts. "Why'd she want to sell?"

"Her children had all moved away, and the house was just too much responsibility. I found the space perfect, and the rest is history."

He followed her down the stairs and across the pavers to a cabana, the kind that was seen along a pool at a luxurious hotel resort. It was covered with drapes that had been tied back in the corners. Inside were a large elevated sectional couch and two lounge chairs.

"Why don't you get comfortable while I start a fire?" Sedona suggested as she walked past him and grabbed a stack of wood.

"Hey, why don't I get that for you?" Keith hurried over and took it from her. "I thought you would have had a gas fire pit."

"Oh no! I love the smell and feel of wood."

"I agree."

Keith put the logs in the large iron bowl. Within

minutes he had a fire roaring and the lights dancing off
of Sedona's lovely face. He took a seat beside her on the
large sectional and it wasn't long before the area
surrounding the cabana was nice and warm. They both
shrugged out of their jackets and he draped them over
one of the lounge chairs.

Sedona was lying on her stomach, staring off into the
fire. She was beautiful.

"Have you ever been in love?" she suddenly asked
out of the blue.

Keith tilted his head, his brows arched in surprise as
he replied, "No, never."

"How'd you manage that?" she asked, eyes sparkling
with curiosity.

He shrugged. "I guess I never stayed in one place
long enough to fall in love. I spent a lot of time at sea.
Women aren't too fond about being with a man who's at
sea nine months out of the year."

"The right woman would be."

He heart thumped. "Then I guess that means I have
something to look forward to." Sedona rolled onto her
back and stared through the draping at the stars
overhead. "I was in love once."

His stomach turned in knots as he stared down at her,
and saw the longing in her eyes. The best thing to do was
to change the subject or even better this would have been
a good time as any to tell her who he was but like he'd
thought before, he'd been hard-headed most of his life.

"What happened?" He felt like the biggest heel
because he already knew. He had been there.

There was a hitch in her breath and her tongue
slipped out as she said, "His name was Derrick. Derrick
Webb." She seemed very small and still. Sedona sat up
against the cushions, shifted her legs, drawing them up

against her chest and wrapped her arms around them comfortingly. His own throat felt tight, making it hard to breath.

"I was attending college and had gone home with my roommate for the weekend. She was from Virginia Beach. Anyway, we were at this popular bar near the beach."

"Mickey's Bar."

She nodded. "Yes, that's the place."

Keith knew the establishment quite well. A hole in the wall frequented by sailors.

She tipped her head and stared up at the treetops, swaying against the dark sky as she continued. "I was sitting at the bar when Derrick came up behind me and whispered in my ear that I was going to be his wife."

Yep. That sounded like something he would do.

"After that we spent every day together until he shipped off to California."

That had been when he and Webb had met, during his tour to California. And then they served together again in Japan, and then that one final deployment that ended both of their careers.

"We fell in love and after two years he proposed." Sedona smiled and stared off into the fire again and he knew she was remembering. Keith searched her face trying to read what she was feeling. "We were supposed to marry after his last deployment, but he died from a fire onboard the ship," she explained, voice shuddering.

Keith swallowed as vivid images surfaced that he quickly pushed away.

"The entire time we were together I was worried he might die in combat, and instead he died in an explosion." Sedona shook her head. "That was probably the worst day of my life."

Mine too. His stomach cramped with thoughts of that

afternoon. Reaching over, he squeezed her arm. "I'm so sorry."

She smiled over at him. "Thank you. It took me a long time to get over his death. I'm going to always love him, but I figured out a while back I needed to let go and get back to the living."

Keith touched her face, his fingers gentle and his voice low and deep. "Sounds like he was one lucky guy."

She nodded, looked at him directly and her next words were choked. "Yeah, he was wasn't he?"

"C'mere." Possessively, Keith brought her over onto his lap and just held her.

"Life doesn't always work out the way we plan it," she said breaking the silence with a shuddered breath.

He slid his hand up and down her arm and shoulder soothingly and kissed her cheek and hair, burning need flooding his chest.

Minutes past and yet neither of them spoke. Instead he listened to the crackling of the fire and the sound of the waterfall feature beating against the rocks. A breeze rustled the trees and he was thankful for the heat coming from the pit.

Sedona lifted her face and her eyes looked luminous in the dark. Leaning forward, he did what felt natural and kissed her.

Sedona was more than ready, meeting his lips halfway and then she started doing something slow and sensual with her tongue that practically short-circuited his brain.

Gently he pressed her back against the cushion and claimed her mouth. He loved the way she whimpered and willingly surrendered, allowing him to take control, causing the blood at his loins to fire hot. The kiss went on for too long, and yet not long enough.

She moaned as he positioned his body on top of hers and deepened the kiss. Damn! He loved the feel of her, soft in the right places, and solid in the rest. Sedona confidently met his strokes and they played together like that for a bit, then finally he skimmed his hand underneath her sweater. He loved the way her body felt, but he wanted more.

The feel of her skin beneath his fingertips unlatched the flood gate. A purr vibrated in Sedona throat. And when he reached for the zipper of her jeans and lowered it, she didn't object. In fact, she hooked her thumbs through the belt loops and tugged them down over her ass followed by her panties.

At the sight of her, Keith shuddered with raw need.

♦ ♦ ♦

"I can't get enough of touching you," he whispered, voice thick with desire.

Neither can I, Sedona thought. *Neither can I.*

His hand grazed across her belly then lowered until one finger threaded slowly through the soft brown curls at her apex.

"You've gotten inside my head," he told her and flicked his thumb over her clit. A deep chuckle rumbled from his throat when Sedona gasped and her hips rocked up to greet him.

"I have?" she moaned.

"Yes, babe, you have." Keith slid a finger along her wet folds then dipped boldly in between, twirling his finger just outside the opening. "You're wet."

No, she was soaked and in a few minutes she hoped to be flooded in ecstasy. She wiggled on the cushions, drawing her body closer and giving him a better angle to penetrate her.

Keith licked his lips and ordered, "Take your sweater off and unfasten your bra."

It took several fumbled attempts before she got the sweater over her head and the lace bra, she popped it free and tossed it away. And as soon as Sedona saw him staring down at her naked body, her heart pumped hard.

"Are you cold?" he said on a sigh, snuggling close.

Cold? His hands all but burned her wherever they touched. "No, I'm burning up."

She lay before him and watched his eyes flow over her chest. Then he finally began to touch. He lifted her breasts one in each hand and began to softly caress. "You have such a beautiful body," he groaned with delight and rolled his thumbs over her nipples. She shivered and gave in to the feeling. He was playing with them, tweaking her nipples causing her body to tighten with each passing second. Damn, he was good at it.

"Your breasts are perfect for my hand and for my mouth." Dipping his head, he sucked a nipple between his lips and she gasped in surprise. Keith teased with his teeth, wrenching a delightful moan from her. He kissed down her belly, nipped at her belly button and inhaled deeply, then he began to lick.

OMG!

Keith's tongue was warm, wet and he had mad skills to say the least. Every stroke brought forth sparks of heat warming her body, and electrifying her. His tongue had the power to rob her of all the strength she had left.

It had been so long time since a man had touched her and she desperately wanted to feel. Alive. Sexy. Desirable. And so freaking aroused. Her libido roared and her nipples throbbed in time with her heartbeat. She didn't care about tomorrow, only what happened now and what she wanted was for him to continue to touch her and to taste her. Keith was confident and skillful. He definitely knew what he was doing.

As his tongue traveled lower, his hands came up and dragged her jeans low enough for her to part her thighs wider and give him better access.

His fingers were warm and long and her body shivered when he spread the folds of her pussy and plunged inside her. They stroked and penetrated causing her to moan, whimper and breathe his name. Desire took over every last reasonable thought in her mind until Sedona couldn't think straight. Not that she really cared. As his fingers pumped inside, the muscles grasped at him, drawing two fingers and then three in deeper. She could feel the fever rising in her blood.

She raised her hips off the cushion. As his fingers delved, her pussy rocked harder, working his fingers in and then out, while his thumb slid up and then down her slippery aroused folds. She whimpered and gyrated her hips, meeting his pumping fingers, thrust for thrust.

An orgasm was so close, she could feel it.

Keith released her nipple from his mouth, and then his tongue painted a path down the length of her.

"I gotta taste you," he said, his warm breath against her skin.

"Keith —"she began, but he shook his head.

"Not a word, not a move, Sedona. Not until you come inside my mouth."

She took a deep breath, her chest expanding as she prepared for him.

Keith bent his head low. His lips kissed the soft flesh between her legs, then he slid his tongue along her folds before dipping inside.

"You taste good," he drawled, hot breath rushing

over her clit.

His fingers had been magical, but his tongue was insane and sent her soaring toward the edge.

"Yes!" she cried. Keith delved deeper. Need coursed through her, demanding the pressure of his tongue to give her release.

He traced lazy circles around her clit and she savored the velvet feel of his tongue. Her pussy throbbed, her clit pulsed hot and hungry for him. It was lust, arousal, she didn't care what it was called, all she knew was Keith was the only man able to give her what she desperately needed. Release. She was sure of it and it threatened to consume her, but she didn't want to let go, not yet. She wanted the feeling to last.

Sedona boldly looked down and caught Keith gazing up at her. He lifted his head slightly and there it was, her juices shimmering at the corner of his lips.

She shivered with pleasure. The sight was such a turn-on!

He went back to work, stroking her clit with his tongue, caressing her ass with his hands. And she was not at all surprised when within minutes her body was shaking. And he knew she was close, she was sure he saw it on her face, heard it in the whimpers and pleas spilling from her lips. Hell yeah, she wanted it. She wanted everything Keith Falcon had to give.

Somehow her legs ended up over his shoulders and there was a wicked twinkle in his eyes, and Sedona knew it was time. Keith drew her clit between his lips again, suckled hungrily, then slid two fingers deep between her folds, in and out, twisting to a rhythm that had her ready to lose her mind.

"Yes, oh yes! That feels so good!" she cried.

Sedona squeezed her eyes shut and bucked beneath

him. No, she didn't want it to end, and yet she didn't know how much more she could take. Her entire body was on high alert, and before she could catch her next breath, Keith applied just enough pressure, shoving her over the edge and her body contracted. All the months of longing, the want and need, exploded into a high-pitched wail of pleasure and a rush of flame.

"Keith!"

Chapter 6

"These measurements are off. Shut it down!"

"What are you talking about?" he said defensively.

Keith swung around and met the ship-fitting mechanic's gaze head-on. "Dale, I'm talking about we're not cutting this steel until we get these calculations right."

"But the production manager already confirmed it," he countered.

"Well, he's wrong. Send the crew up to the bow of the ship to help Finch. In the meantime, the project down here is on hold until an engineer comes in and takes a look at these measurements." Without another word he turned and walked away.

"Where are you going?" Dale called after him.

Keith didn't even bother to turn around as he said, "I've gotta plane to catch."

With that, he departed the berthing space on the ship and headed toward the gangway through the security checkpoint.

They'd been going back and forth for the last week over the calculations and something had told him the evening crew was going to get the measurements wrong. He wasn't at all surprised to have received a call at four o'clock from the evening supervisor pleading with him to drop by before he caught the plane to Jacksonville. Sure enough, they were off about three inches which was a lot more than legally permitted in his book. And until the cuts were precise, work was on hold and the crew could go ahead and start their holiday weekend.

Keith dragged an irritated hand down his face. What in the world were they thinking? This wasn't just any ship. They were talking about a military aircraft vessel. The placement of the gun mount was crucial; the weapon had to be cocked at the precise angle or else...

He erased that possibility from his mind and unlike the night supervisor he wasn't interested in taking any unnecessary chances. Keith had a reputation of being good at his job, and he'd be damned before he'd be responsible for any careless mistakes.

As he headed across the yard, he remembered the earplugs and removed them from his ears, and slipped them into his pocket just as a beautiful woman was heading his way that reminded him of Sedona. Same brown skin and dark wavy hair, only difference was the woman was short and wearing a naval uniform. He nodded as he passed and drew a deep breath.

Even when he shut his eyes for bed Tuesday night he saw her, and all day yesterday, Sedona had been the subject of a constant erection. Keith inhaled sharply and tried to simmer the fire brewing at his crotch. It wasn't easy. All he could think about was kissing her lips, holding her body beneath his hands, and his tongue on her clit that smelled so good. The scent was still in his head, driving him over the edge. It was the guilt tightening at his gut that had Keith second-guessing every decision he'd made since they'd first met on Sunday.

Sedona was beautiful, talented and everything a man could ever ask for and he was lying to her. Knowing that gnawed at his conscience. He had always been a man of integrity. He prided himself on it and yet here he was being less than truthful to a woman he was aching to claim as his own.

Tuesday night under the cabana, it had taken everything he had to leave her. The entire ride home, Keith heard her soft breaths and whimpers with her legs up over his shoulders. Just thinking about the way she had thrashed around on the cushions had left him horny and so painfully aroused he'd laid awake most of the night only to finally fall asleep due to exhaustion.

As he moved toward his car, Keith cleared his throat and made another attempt at controlling his emotions. They were surging strongly. One was an impulse to drive over to Sedona's, lift her into his arms, and finish what they'd started Tuesday night.

But one thing for certain, he had no regrets. Keith had already made up his mind she was going to be his. There was something powerful about her that was drawing him to her. It was the same for her as well. The whimpers, the desire in her eyes; both confirmed her reaction, and told him everything he needed to know. They belonged together.

It was maddening, he thought with a shake of the head but he now understood why Webb had loved her so much. Sedona was truly irresistible. And that's why he'd decided to put some distance between them until he figured out how to tell her the truth.

Unfortunately, he had a feeling it was already too late.

◆ ◆ ◆

Sedona was speeding down I-64, going at almost eighty miles an hour. She loved her car. After starting her own company and proving to be successful at what she did, she decided to reward herself for all the hard work and determination.

Sirius XM music was playing one love song after another. How fitting? Especially since she couldn't get Keith off her mind. Tuesday night had been mind-boggling. Never had she experienced an evening filled with laughter and sensual pleasure. Just thinking about his tongue between her thighs had her squeezing her legs tightly together on the seat.

Keith had come into her life at just the right time.

As she listened to Jodeci sing, "Every Moment", Sedona thought about every second of their dates. How in the world had a man so amazing managed to stay single? She wondered. Sure he explained being out at sea made it impossible, but she felt there had to be more. Or maybe it was just her good fortune, she thought with a salacious grin. She definitely felt lucky to have met a man who was not only an amazing kisser, but knew other unique ways to use his tongue.

At the close of their evening, Keith had kissed her and then went home. The next day, Sedona waited to hear from him, and being the stubborn woman she was, she didn't text or call even though she had been checking her phone ever since.

Nothing.

It was just as well. They needed to take whatever was happening between them slowly. Besides, Keith was on a plane headed to Jacksonville. She didn't expect to hear from him while he was out of town, but a part of her couldn't help but hope that she would.

Her phone chirped in her ear. Heart pounding, she reached down for her phone and glanced briefly at the screen, hoping it was Keith, but instead she smiled when she realized it was Bianca. They had been playing phone tag all week.

Sedona pressed the button to activate her Bluetooth. "Hey, Bianca."

"Hey! All set for Thanksgiving?"

She could already taste her mother's homemade pecan pies. "I'm headed to Richmond and I'm starving."

"Why didn't you grab something to eat?"

Giggling, she replied, "I'm trying to save my appetite, so I had a granola bar and coffee this morning."

"Sounds like you're going to be a starving bitch by the time you make it there."

Sedona released a fit of laughter. "I'm sure I will be, but you know my mom throws down in the kitchen."

"Yes, she does. I wish I could say the same about my mother." Bianca laughed. She was right. Aunt Jessica wouldn't dare spend the day in the kitchen ruining her nails. "You make sure you tell Aunt Bettye I said, Happy Thanksgiving."

"And you tell everyone I said, Happy Thanksgiving." Her family was having dinner at her brother Jabarie's house.

"I will. Okay, so the reason why I'm calling is to find out how lunch went with Mr. Golden Graham?"

Sedona exploded with laughter. "*Golden Graham*, really?"

Bianca giggled right along with her. "Donie, as golden brown as he was in those photos, I didn't know what else to call him. Anyway, hurry with the details."

"What do you want to know?" she said and grinned.

"Everything, Sedona, quit playing! Was he as handsome as he looked in his photographs because you know men like to post pictures that are ten years old, long before the receding hairline and potbellies?"

She gave a rude snort. "Does London have either of

those things?"

"Not my husband," Bianca said defensively. "He's still just as handsome as he was the day I met him."

Sedona leaned her head back against the headrest and noted the warm shiver of delight raining down her spine. "Keith is tall and handsome with a gorgeous face that I don't think I could ever get tired of staring at."

Bianca must have heard something in the tone of her voice because she replied, "Ooh, sounds to me like you like him. Quit stalling! I want details."

Sedona laughed and while she took exit twenty toward Richmond, she told her cousin about her two encounters with Keith. She hadn't realized how badly she had wanted someone to talk to and share all the details. Speaking their relationship into existence gave her a chance to really reflect on everything that had happened in only two dates. Two mind-boggling, lip-smacking dates.

"Couples roller skating? How romantic is that?"

"I know," Sedona replied with a shaky breath. "It was really something. I haven't done that in a long time."

"I just bet. And what else did you do that you haven't done in a while."

Leave it to her cousin to get straight to the point. "Now you're being nosy."

"I can't help it if I want details, especially since it was me who had you set up the profile."

"Hmmm, I wonder what London would say if I told him that," Sedona teased.

"Don't even think about it."

"Then stay in your lane. This is my love life not yours."

"Love life? Oooh, do tell! Sounds like you did a lot more than just kissing."

Grinning, Sedona replied, "Who said the only thing he kissed was my lips?"

Bianca started screaming in her ear. Sedona lowered the volume on the Bluetooth. "You finished yet?" she asked and waited for her cousin to pull herself together. What was it with married women trying to live vicariously through single women? She wondered.

"Yes, I'm finished. I can't believe you let him..." Bianca gasped and then started laughing again.

"You sure know how to make a woman feel self-conscious."

"Why? You're young and beautiful. There's nothing to be ashamed of."

No, shame was the last thing on Sedona's mind. If anything she was dying for an encore.

"When are you going to see him again?"

Sedona frowned and was glad her cousin couldn't see. "I don't know."

"What do you mean?" There was a slight pause. "Have you spoken to him?"

"Nope."

There was another pause. "Have you tried calling him?"

Her eyes darted to her side-view mirror as she replied, "No, of course not."

Bianca was quiet for a moment longer, then let loose a long-suffering sigh. "You lecture about women feeling empowered and taking the reins...I don't get it. What's wrong with you taking the driver's seat?"

"Because I want a man to want me enough he's willing to chase me just a little bit," Sedona admitted.

"Really cuz?" Bianca said with a laugh.

"Why are you laughing? Webb chased me."

Bianca gave a rude snort. "Sure, from across the

ocean! The relationship was long distance. He had no choice."

"And what's wrong with that?" she retorted.

"What's wrong is nowadays you have to at least let the man know you're interested. Have you done that?"

"I think I have," Sedona replied, as she remembered how willingly she had opened her legs and allowed him to feast.

"You know I used to listen to my brothers, especially Jace, talking about women playing hard to get and he's right. We do. Like you said, we love the chase but men like to be chased just a little bit, too."

"Mom taught Sage and I to never run after a man," she reminded.

"True, but at least give the man a hint."

Suddenly, Sedona's salacious mind was buzzing with ideas. She released a long breath. "You're right. I'll text him."

"Good, and then if you don't hear from him, well…, you can at least chalk it up to a good tongue-licking."

Tears were trickling from the corners of her eyes, she was laughing so hard.

"Hey, I'm just saying…" Bianca giggled.

They talked until she drew near the airport and the phone signal weakened. Sedona promised to keep Bianca posted and hung up. Reaching down, she changed the music and stopped when she heard Jill Scott bellowing through the speakers.

Shivers of anticipation trickled along her spine. Sedona really wanted to see Keith Falcon again and she was not about to let pride stand in her way. As soon as she arrived at her parents, she planned to break the silence and send him a text message.

Chapter 7

Sedona hung her coat in a closet in the foyer of her parent's sprawling house and headed to the rear where she heard laughter. The family room was one of her favorite rooms. With twelve-foot ceilings, her mother had spared no expense. Colorful handwoven rugs were across the dark wood flooring and tapestries covered the couches and chairs inside the massive room that had floor to ceiling windows that looked out onto a professionally landscaped yard.

"Hey everyone!" Sedona said merrily and sauntered into the room.

"About time you got your big head here!" her brother Rance teased.

Playfully, she rolled her eyes at the NBA player before he engulfed her in the circle of his large arms. "Hey Donie. How you been?"

She gave him a big hug, then tilted her head back to meet his dark sable-brown gaze. "Can't complain." He kissed her cheek, then Sedona released him and made her way across the room and over to her mother who wore a concerned frown on her almond face.

"Sedona, you look like you've lost weight."

She blew out a long breath and decided to hug her mother's tall, athletic frame instead of commenting. It was always the same thing.

"Did you have breakfast this morning?" Bettye Beaumont—who worked out religiously five days a week—drew back from the embrace, her amber eyes critical.

"Mom, I'm fine…, really." She gave her a reassuring look, then caught movement out of the corner of her eyes. "Reese!" Glad for the distraction, Sedona raced over to her big brother and threw her arms over his shoulders.

"Hey Donie."

"When did you get in?" she asked and leaned back, staring up at his toasted-almond-colored face and smiled.

"We arrived late last night." He kissed her cheek. Reese had been living in Hawaii for almost two years where his wife Dominique was the human resources manager for the Beaumont Waikiki Hotel. Reese had once been one of the top thoracic surgeons in the country until a car accident ended his career, but over the last year he seemed satisfied with being an instructor at a teaching hospital in Waikiki.

Sedona spotted his wife sauntering into the room in a black pants suit that embraced all her voluptuous curves.

"Hey!" Dominique shrieked. She hurried over and wrapped her arms around her neck. "How are you? Where the hell did you find those boots?"

Sedona beamed at the beauty with her smooth, coffee complexion and short spiky dark hair as she said, "The outlet mall at Rehoboth."

Reese groaned. "Oh no! Don't tell her that. Then she's going to insist on making that drive."

Dominique playfully slugged her husband in the arm. "We were going up to visit Jace and Sheyna anyway, so what's wrong with driving an additional ten miles?"

"Ten miles means ten hours of shopping." He brushed his hand across a neatly trimmed goatee.

Sedona giggled. "I'm sure Sheyna will be more than happy to go with you."

Reese mumbled something under his breath causing the two women to laugh.

"Where's Debra and my little Reese's Peanut Butter Cup?" She looked from one to the other curiously. Reese beamed with pride at the mention of his nephew. The popular candy bar had also been his nickname growing up.

Dominique pointed toward the kitchen. "They're in the kitchen with your father."

She chatted a few more minutes, then wandered down the hall and into the large kitchen that was a chef's dream. Rance's wife, Debra, was sitting at the island with her son, Tyrese Christopher Beaumont cradled to her shoulder. Richard Beaumont was standing in front of the stove, carving a fried turkey.

"Hi Sedona!" Debra said when she spotted Sedona stepping into the kitchen.

She sauntered over and kissed her sister-in-law on her smooth butterscotch-colored cheek. "Ooh, can I hold him?"

"Of course you can." Debra gently handed him to her and as soon as Sedona stared down at his face she drew in a slow breath.

"Oh, he is so handsome," she cooed. "Look at my little Reesie."

"Girl, don't let Rance hear you call him Reesie. You should have seen the look he gave Dominique."

She cradled her nephew against her chest and spat, "I'm not thinking about my brother." She turned and stepped over to her father. "Hey Dad."

Richard Beaumont stopped carving long enough to lean over and kiss his oldest daughter on her cheek. "Hello Donie." A broad smile swept across his lips. One look at the man's dark complexion and sable eyes, and you knew he was a Beaumont and the founder of the Beaumont Automotive Group.

Her father began his first Toyota dealership before Sedona was born, then the company grew to become one of the largest auto sales groups on the East Coast. Her father knew early on expansion was one way of staying ahead of the competition. After Toyota he became Ford, Lincoln, BMW, Mercedes, Nissan and Volkswagen with nearly two dozen Beaumont dealerships.

"That turkey is looking good," she complimented, then snatched a piece and put it in her mouth before her father could stop her.

It was a tradition that every year their father fried one turkey while her mother made another the old-fashioned way, stuffed with homemade dressing.

"I see you're empty-handed. You didn't bring a dish?"

Debra laughed and Sedona joined in.

"Dad I don't know why it's hard for you to understand I don't have time to cook. That's why I'm always coming to see you and Mom."

Standing at six-eight, he towered over Sedona as he shook his salt and pepper head. "I don't know how you think you're going to snag yourself a husband if you can't cook."

"There are other ways," Sedona said with a saucy grin that she knew would make her father roll his eyes toward heaven, praying for strength. "Like beauty and brains."

She rocked her nephew in her arms and was preparing to hear her father's lecture on lasting relationships when the youngest Beaumont, Remy, came plowing into the kitchen.

"Whassup Fam!" the radio personality cried as if he

was still on the air.

"Hey Remy," the three chorused. He then engulfed the ladies with his muscular arms and placed a gentle kiss to his nephew's cheek.

Sedona playfully rolled her eyes. "Dad, instead of lecturing me about relationships, this is the person you need to be talking about."

"Relationships? Oh no!" Remy held up the sign of the cross as if he was swearing off a vampire. "We ain't having any of that."

Debra laughed while Sedona and her father shared a look.

Remy was known as Dr. Feel. He loved the ladies as long as the situation "feels" good, but the second she tried to put on the chains he would be off to the next beautiful honey. He was the co-host of the nationally syndicated radio program, *He vs. She* that was heard by thousands of viewers across the country. He was all about dating and loving life as a bachelor. A committed relationship was the last thing Remy wanted.

"I caught part of your show last night," Sedona commented.

He gave a cocky grin. "*Why men get bored in bed?* Yeah last night our phones were ringing off the hook."

Debra's big brownish-green eyes bulged wide as she studied Remy. "I can only imagine what came out of your mouth."

Sedona loved getting a rise out of her brother. "Deb, he had the nerve to say it was up to women to keep things interesting in the bedroom."

Her mouth dropped open.

Sedona heard Pops mumble something under his breath and she chuckled lightly. Remy was definitely a piece of work. But the twenty-five year old was so handsome she could see why the women were falling at his feet. Tall and toasted brown, he took after their mother with his Samoan features. Strong nose, high cheekbones, and as usual he had his long wavy shoulder-length hair pulled back with a leather strap.

The others started gathering in the kitchen and got into a heated discussion over the show's topic. Mom filled trays with ranch dressing and pulled out the appetizers. Sedona gave her nephew to his father and was eating deviled eggs and laughing at Remy acting a fool when Rush and Roman stepped into the kitchen. While everyone exchanged greetings she admired her brothers. They were all tall, although Rance a.k.a. Dr. Dribble was the tallest at seven-two. Roman, a few inches shorter, played football in high school before pursuing a career in dentistry. After her father suffered a heart attack, he stepped back from the day-to-day operations and handed over the reins to Rush who was now the CEO of the Beaumont Automotive Group. He had a doctoral degree in organizational management and since taking over had expanded the group by adding five new locations.

"I have an announcement," Rance said, then rose from the chair, drawing the attention of his family. "My beautiful wife here will never say anything but—"

"Rance," Debra cut in and tried to communicate something with her eyes but he smiled and squeezed her shoulder lovingly before continuing.

"*DebbieCakes* won Bakery of the Year for the state of Delaware."

"What?" Sedona clapped her hands. "Oh that is wonderful!"

Reese picked up his glass and gave a small salute. "I'm not surprised. Your cupcakes are worth the drive."

Debra blushed and dropped her head briefly to her lap and back up again sending her wavy honey-brown hair spiraling around her face. "Thank you, I was so shocked when I found out."

"The mayor of Sheraton Beach came out with the media and presented her with an award that is now hanging in the store's window." Rance looked lovingly at his wife who was holding their son in her arms.

"We're so proud of you," her mother said and then each of the others chimed in. Sedona watched her brother, standing proudly beside his wife. *I want that*, she thought as a wave of envy ruffled her stomach.

The family chatted, nonstop, the way they always did while gathered in the kitchen. Her mother removed a spiral ham from the oven and then the women carried everything into the next room and placed it on a large dining room table which allowed plenty of room for their family. Sedona was carrying a plate of cranberry sauce to the table when her grandmother shuffled into the dining room.

"Nan!" she cried, then hurried to put the dish on the table and walked over and wrapped her arms around the tiny woman's frail body.

"There you are." She said and when she released her, Nan took her hand. "Come. I want to talk to you."

Puzzled, she followed her into the living room and patted the seat beside her on the custom blue couch. As soon as they were both seated she stared adoringly at the eighty-two-year-old Samoan woman who still drove herself to church every Sunday.

"What's wrong Nan?"

The wrinkles on her almond face appeared to smooth whenever she smiled. "I dreamed you were pregnant."

"*Pregnant?*" Sedona chirped and then she started

laughing. "I'm not pregnant, Nan."

"I didn't say it was now," she grumbled with a dismissive wave. "I saw this happening in the future."

Sedona frowned. "Nan, I need a man to get pregnant."

"You mean sex?"

She struggled to keep a straight face. The last thing she wanted to do was discuss her sex life with her grandmother. "Yes, Nan."

"What are you waiting on? A beautiful woman like you should have men lined up at the door." Nan arched an inquisitive brow.

With a laugh, Sedona leaned back onto the cushions of the couch. "Well I don't know about that, but I've met a few interesting men."

Nan's eyes sparked with interest. "Then that's a start. Now we just need to get one of them to convince you to make some babies. There are seven of you and so far we only have one little person running around this house."

She groaned because Nan was starting to sound like her mother. "I'm sure Reese is next."

A smile curled her painted red lips. "Let's hope so." They both turned to find Rush's tall frame, towering in the entryway.

"Hey you two, Mom is ready to get started."

"Okay." Sedona rose and helped Nan to her feet. "Don't worry Nan. I hope to someday marry and make lots of babies." Her mind wandered to Keith. *I wonder if he wants the same.*

Nan patted her with her small hand. "Hopefully it will happen during my lifetime."

"Nan, I think you're going to be around for a long, long time." Leaning forward she kissed her warm cheek and followed her into the dining room.

Sedona moved to her seat beside Remy and joined hands for prayer.

"May we bow our heads?" her father said from the head of the table.

Sedona closed her eyes and heard running feet coming down the wooden foyer.

"Sorry I'm late!"

Everyone looked up and turned. Her younger sister Sage was walking across the room while shrugging out of a short, black leather bomber jacket. Her jean-clad legs were covered starting at mid-thigh by a pair of leather black stiletto boots. A form-fitting sweater had Delicious in rhinestones across her breasts.

"What else is new?" Remy muttered under his breath.

"Bite me, Remy," Sage spat as she came around and moved to her space beside Sedona at the table. "I was working on an engine and it took longer than I had scheduled."

A slight frown marred her mother's forehead as she said, "I don't know why you insist on getting your hands all grimy."

"It's what I do Mom."

"But it's Thanksgiving. The dealership is supposed to be closed."

Her father cleared his throat. "Can we say grace, please?"

With a smirk, Sage shared a conspiratorial look with Sedona, then bowed her head. Leave it to her father to know when an argument was brewing. Her mother never understood why her youngest decided to pursue a career as an auto mechanic before going on to earn a double major in mechanical engineering and business management. Sage was currently working on an MBA at Virginia Commonwealth University.

As soon as the prayer was complete, the family lowered to their seats and started passing the serving dishes around the table.

"Hey Gigi."

Sage turned her head sending the large hoop earrings dangling from her lobes swinging. "Hi Donie. When did you get in?"

"I drove down this afternoon. I tried calling you."

She blew out a breath. "We had so many cars at the garage, I decided to get a head start."

Sage managed both of the Beaumont Collision Centers as well as was the general manager of two of their dealerships—Mercedes Benz and Hyundai. As her sister spooned green beans onto her plate, she glanced down at her nails, although clean, they were cut low. Not at all like the French tips Sedona couldn't imagine going without.

"You should have known Mom was going to be pissed."

"She'll get over it," Sage replied. But Sedona noticed how her sister lowered her voice and said in a soft, pleading voice, "You need to help me convince Dad to let me run the dealerships in Fredericksburg and Charlottesville."

When her father decided it was time for a break from running the day-to-day operations, his first choice had been Rush, and Sage had been salty ever since. Dr. Fix-It believed she was more capable than anyone else, and ran circles around her brothers when it came to working under the hood.

Sedona noted the mischievous grin curling her sister's painted lips and shook her head. "Uh-uh, I'm not getting into that fight. Why don't you just ask Rush?"

Sage exhaled slowly as she sliced a knife into a piece

of turkey. "He's just as bad as Dad. Neither one of them think I can handle it, but what they fail to recognize is my dealerships have been the top performers for the last three quarters."

She had to agree. Her sister was hungry and driven, a natural born salesman. Unlike her, Sage loved being a part of the dealership, whereas her father had to make Sedona work there. Even then she preferred to work in the office while Sage was out on the floor selling cars when she was just fifteen. By the time she had her driver's license, Sage had already started tinkering under the hood.

Sedona took in Sage's wide smile below high cheekbones. The dark beauty had burgundy tinted hair with blunt cut bangs, the sides dangling down past her chin on one side and her shoulder on the other. It was a playful, yet edgy new look.

"Dad, I sold that CLK we had in the showroom," she announced loud enough for everyone to hear.

His eyes twinkled with pleasure. "Really? Gigi that's wonderful."

"I gave her the referral," Roman mumbled with his mouth full.

Sage scowled and worked to keep a measure of calm as she ran a hand across her chin. "What does it matter?"

"Congratulations," Rance replied. He'd always had a soft spot for his baby sister.

She blew him a kiss. "Thank you, Rance."

While they ate, the family went back and forth with one topic after another, some causing the table to get a little loud and obnoxious, especially when Sage commented that now that Tony Romo was out for the season, the Carolina Panthers had a shot at winning the Super Bowl.

Remy snapped his fingers. "This is a Cowboy's house. Why the hell are we talking about the Panthers?"

"Remy, watch your mouth!" her mother scolded. And then the rest of the wild bunch chimed in with their crude comments. Sage glanced over at her and winked. Sedona shook her head. Her little sister was a mess. As she ate, her mind wandered back to Keith, wondering how his holiday was going and if he could fit in with her family.

She grinned because even though they had just met, she had a warm feeling he wouldn't have a problem fitting in at all.

♦ ♦ ♦

"There's peach pie and ice cream."

Keith rubbed his stomach and groaned. "Grandma, I'm too stuffed."

The small round nutty-brown colored woman smiled lovingly up at him. "Well, it's there when you're good and ready."

"I definitely plan on having a piece." He leaned over, kissed her warm brown cheek then excused himself and went downstairs where most of the men of the family were kicked back, sipping beers and watching the football game. The Bears and Packers were playing. The Cowboys would be playing against the Panthers later. The men were being crude and raunchy as usual. He moved over to the bar where his cousin, Nate was seated.

"Who's winning?" he asked.

"The Bears are up by ten. They just had an eighty-yard drive," he answered without even bothering to look up.

"Damn," Keith mumbled as he grabbed a glass,

moved behind the bar and reached for the vodka, followed by the vermouth. He made a martini, then took a seat on a barstool just as the Packers intercepted the ball. His father, a diehard Bears fan, was out of his seat cussing like a retired Navy commander.

Keith chuckled and started following the game. His cousin Jason and his wife were seated together on a loveseat in the corner both wearing Packers jerseys. Kenyatta talked shit and understood football better than any woman he'd ever met. He admired her spunk and sophistication. It had taken Jason five years to get her to marry him and he hadn't regretted a moment of it. Sedona came to mind and Keith shifted on the stool. The last thing he needed was a hard-on in a roomful of men even though they were all family.

"C'mon, throw the damn ball!" He heard his grandfather grumble and Keith chuckled. Good thing his grandmother was upstairs, otherwise she'd swear he was raising his blood pressure. Keith smiled as he thought about the couple who had been married more than sixty-five years. Uncle Frank who was sitting beside him on the oversized sofa, was working on close to fifty years of marriage with Aunt Pam and Nate's mom, Ginger, was also getting ready to celebrate twenty-five years with Mr. Pete. There was a great deal of longevity in the room. Unfortunately his own parents divorced when he was ten. His father still hadn't remarried, instead Keith Sr. was partying and dating women half his age. He had no immediate interest for another ball and chain, so he said. His mother, on the other hand, had remarried and was living in Charlottesville with his stepfather. They had just celebrated twenty years.

Keith still remembered when his parents sat him down and told him they were ending their marriage.

He'd cried like a baby, and when his father moved out he thought if he made him proud, he would come back home, so Keith decided to join the Navy like his father. He prepared for it — working out and joining a swim team, all with the hopes of becoming a Navy Seal, and pleasing his father. As soon as he'd turned eighteen, he'd rushed to the recruiting office and joined. Only his backstroke wasn't strong enough and he wasn't qualified to be a Seal. His father had refused to let him quit and told Keith to follow his own heart. By then Keith had realized his parents were never getting back together, especially since his mother had already remarried, and his father seemed happy with a different woman each week. Keith finally decided to live his own life and he didn't care if he wasn't a Seal, just as long as he was a sailor. He'd loved every moment of it and had planned on staying in the Navy until he either aged out or was kicked out, whichever happened first. He just never expected the latter to happen before he had put in twenty years toward retirement.

Keith took a sip from the martini glass as he relived the scene that had haunted him for months — the explosion on the ship. The day Webb lost his life and while trying to save him, a metal bulkhead had fallen and sliced through his ankle. No amount of surgeries would ever repair it. It rarely hurt now except when it rained or he'd been on his feet for too many hours but according to the Navy, Keith was non-deployable and no longer fit for duty.

Thank you for your service.

Have a nice life.

After Keith was discharged, he'd returned to Jacksonville and spent months feeling sorry for himself before one afternoon he caught his reflection in the mirror and saw his disheveled appearance. The next day he'd applied at all of the shipyards, landed a job in Portsmouth, and the rest was history.

In the last year, Keith had settled into a life in Newport News that had become a routine — work, home, bed. But a few months ago, he decided he'd wanted more. Being a bachelor started to suck. He wanted someone to come home to. Someone to share his life. A son to carry on the Falcon family name. None of the women he'd met at the bars were good enough to take home to Mama. He figured there had to be a woman out there who'd want the same.

Nate's phone buzzed. He reached inside his front pocket, stared down at the incoming text, smiled, and then quickly typed a response.

"New chick in your life?"

His head came up. "Nah, I've been kicking it with Cindy for about four months now. I think she might be the one. Smart, beautiful personality and educated," Nate added with a smile.

"She sounds like all the others," Keith said, teasingly.

"Nah, this one is different," he admitted with a far off look in his eyes and went back to sipping his beer.

"How so?"

Nate swiveled slightly on the stool and faced him. "Cuz, I can't describe it. There's just something about her. Man, the connection is off the chain. Shit...I can't explain."

"I get it." Keith admitted between sips. "I met a female and have the same vibe with her. Hell, I hear her voice over the phone and it makes my dick hard," he added and the two chuckled. "I'm really feeling her but I'm not sure how far I'm gonna be able to take us."

"Why?"

"Remember my boy Webb?"

Nate nodded. "Yeah, the one who died in the fire?"

"Yep that's him. Well, Sedona was his fiancée."

"Oh snap!" Nate started laughing. "How the hell did that happen?"

Keith shrugged. "I met her online and couldn't help myself." He whipped out his phone and logged onto the site and pulled up Sedona's profile. Nate took one look at her and whistled.

"Damn, I don't blame you. She's fine! Looks like she's from the islands."

Grinning, Keith looked down at her photograph and his heart picked up tempo. "Yeah, she's half Samoan. Mother was born on an island near Hawaii."

Nate smiled. "I can tell you're really feeling her."

He was too damn observant. But he was right. It had been a long time since the mere sight of a woman had aroused him physically. "Yeah, I'm definitely feeling her."

"Then what's the problem?"

"I haven't gotten around to telling her who I am," he conceded, then scowled.

Nate shot him an incredulous look. "Oh snap! Dude, you're starting a relationship with a lie."

"I never lied."

Nate's brow rose. "No, but you haven't told her the truth either."

Keith felt an uncomfortable prickling down his spine. "I know and that's the problem. I'm afraid if I tell her now she won't have anything to do with me."

"True. But if you don't say anything and she finds out later…"Nate warned.

That's what he was worried about.

Chapter 8

Sedona was just pulling into her driveway when her cell phone buzzed. She climbed out, fumbled inside her purse and answered the call before it went to voicemail.

"Hello?"

"Hey."

As soon as she heard Keith's deep, nipple-raising voice, her insides quivered and she couldn't resist the smile curling her lips. "Hi Keith."

"How was your Thanksgiving?"

"It was wonderful!" she said as she slammed the car door and lowered the garage door.

"What's that noise?"

"Oh." She forgot he could hear that. "That's the garage. I'm just getting home."

"Oh, my bad. You want me to call you later?"

"No," she said and then scolded herself for sounding so eager. "I'm good. Really." She stepped into the house and Cocoa rushed toward her. Sedona set her purse on the island then reached down and stroked her cat. "How was your holiday?"

"It was good, but for some reason I couldn't get this amazing woman I met off my mind."

Her smile broadened. "A woman, huh? She must have made some impression." She could hear the flirting creeping into her voice.

"She did. That's why I can't stop thinking about her."

"And neither can she," Sedona blurted, but wasn't as angry as she would have thought. Suddenly she wanted him to know what she was thinking and feeling because whatever it was, it wasn't going away. Cocoa scurried away and Sedona rose and took a seat on one of the leather barstools at her kitchen island. "Did you get my text?" She had sent a message she looked forward to seeing him again.

"Yes and I need to see you."

Yes! Sedona started kicking her legs with excitement then stopped. "I'd like that. When would you like to see me?"

"Now," Keith replied and she swore he growled. "I need to see you now."

"Okay."

"I'll give you enough time to unpack and settle in. How's seven? I can pick up a Red Box movie."

Sedona was sure Keith could hear the smile in her voice. "Sounds good. I'll pop some buffalo wings in the oven. I also have chips and dip unless you want something else"

"No, babe. All that matters is I get to see you. Anything else is just an added bonus."

Her stomach quivered. Keith knew exactly what to say. "I'll see you then."

After she ended the call, Sedona went back out into the garage to retrieve her rolling overnight luggage and carried it up to her room. There were so many emotions inside her head, she had to stop and take a seat on the edge of the bed and catch her breath. When was the last time a man made her feel wild and crazy? Webb? Maybe, but not at this level of intensity. She had always believed what she and Webb had was unique and special. But what she felt when she was around Keith — or merely when she heard his voice—was a feeling she had never experienced before and she liked it. She liked it a lot.

She unpacked her suitcase, then hurried to shower and change into something comfortable. It was barely five so she had time to take a short nap, even though Sedona had a feeling sleep wasn't going to come easy. Surprisingly, as soon as she lay across the bed, wrapped in the thirsty bath towel, she dozed off. Thank goodness she had set her alarm.

By seven, Sedona put the wings in the oven, had a bottle of red wine chilling and was dressed in black leggings and a yellow sweater. She was ready and shaking with anticipation. She put her iPhone onto the docking station and decided on soft jazz instead of slow R&B.

By the time the doorbell rang, she practically raced to the door. Please Lord, let him be the one," she silently prayed, because if not her heart was headed for trouble.

◆ ◆ ◆

Keith's memory had not done her justice. Sedona was beautiful, sexy and a driving need to possess her pulled at his chest. He had been right. Everything he had been feeling was there burning right at the forefront of his mind.

"Hi," she said shyly.

"Hello Sedona," he replied and when she stepped aside, Keith entered into the house.

"It's cold tonight," she said.

He nodded, reached out, sweeping his arm around her waist and drew her to him. Leaning forward, he kissed her gently at first, then he deepened the kiss, sliding his tongue over hers. "I couldn't wait to do that again."

When he pulled away, she drew in a shuddering breath. "Me either."

"Well in that case..."he brought his mouth over hers again.

Warm lips collided with his. And there was hunger, plenty of it coming from him and from Sedona's mouth. He threaded his fingers into her hair as he claimed her mouth and when she moaned, the sound dissolved any rational thoughts he had left.

The need to breathe was the only reason Keith finally drew back. He wanted her in ways he hadn't wanted a woman in a long, long time. Correction...He wanted her in ways that had nothing to do with lust and everything to do with need. Staring down at her beautiful face, he watched as Sedona's eyes slowly opened. Her tongue slipped out to wet her lips and he felt his cock shifting in his jeans.

"Damn, you sure know how to make a girl feel missed."

"Sweetheart, you have no idea." Not sure he wanted her to know he was aroused, Keith winked, then released her. "Before we watch the movie, how about a tour of your home?"

She looked pleased and he was grateful because he was two seconds away from dragging her into his arms again and having his way with her. Sedona was just as aroused as he was. Her hardened nipples were straining against the cashmere sweater.

"Come this way." She led him through one room after another.

The house had an impressive open concept. The floors were covered in dark red Moroccan wood and the exposed beams in all of the rooms downstairs had been stained an identical hue. Her taste in furniture was interesting. None of the pieces matched and yet it had a nice artsy vibe that was definitely Sedona's style. There were four bedrooms upstairs. Keith stepped into a master bedroom that was covered in rich beige carpeting. His mouth began to salivate when he spotted the massive bed at the center that looked feminine and so damn inviting. As he thought of all the wicked things he wanted to do with her, his loins throbbed again with need. The rest of the tour was a blur because he couldn't get that damn bed out of his head. By the time they made it back downstairs to the large galley style kitchen, he was ready to curl up on the couch and hold her in his arms.

Sedona reached for an oven mitt. "Chips and dip are there. Plates are over here. Let me get the wings out of the oven."

Keith couldn't move as he watched Sedona lean over and remove the tray. *Damn*, the shape of her round ass in leggings was torture.

He was desperate to change the subject. "I took the scenic route over here. This is really a great neighborhood."

"It's called Wythe. It was named after one of the original signers of the Declaration of Independence. Charming architecture and lovely waterside view, it's a lot of house for one person, but I like it."

"And it suits you. Your taste and style is stamped all over this house. Now wait until you see my townhouse. Everything is just the way it was when I bought it. White walls, cheap carpeting on the floor," he chuckled when Sedona scrunched up her face in response. "I figured I would get that kind of reaction." He reached for a chip and dipped it into the salsa as he said, "Everyone doesn't have your talent."

"What talents? I'm good with colors and I love to shop. That's as far as the talents go." She smiled and reached inside the bowl for a chip and took a bite. "No, in all seriousness, my mother was an interior designer, so I think some of it may just come naturally."

"Aha! I knew there was a reason."

Giggling, Sedona carried the tray of wings over to the island and then reached for the cork screw. "I hope you like red."

He frowned. "I prefer a beer, but I can drink red."

Sedona's brow rose as if she suddenly remembered something. "Wait, you might be in luck." She scurried across the espresso-travertine tiled floor over to a large stainless steel refrigerator and looked inside. "My brother was here a few weeks ago and brought a six pack and left two."

Sedona held up the bottle, then walked over and rummaged in a drawer for a bottle opener. While her back was turned, Keith's gaze rolled up and down the length of her. She was truly a beautiful woman.

"Here you go," she said and he took the bottle from her hand.

"Thanks."

Smiling, she reached for a flute and then filled it with wine before returning to her seat at the island. "So...tell me about your family. Is your father still in the Navy?" she asked and reached for a wing.

"Oh no! He did twenty-five years before he took over my grandfather's dry cleaning business."

"That's amazing. I've lived in Virginia my entire life and none of my five brothers ever had any desire to join the military."

"Really?"

She nodded. "My cousin Jaden joined the Army for a short stint then he went on to open a string of auto body shops."

Keith nodded knowingly. "AutoBeau right?"

She blinked her eyes flirtatiously and said, "Are you stalking me?"

He tossed his head back with laughter. "Your family is famous. Who doesn't know who the Beaumonts are? A hotel chain...an auto dealership...auto body shop and then there is the marriage to Clarence's Chicken & Fish House. I feel privileged just to be in your presence."

She gave a rude snort and tossed a chicken bone at him. Keith had such a great sense of humor he laughed right along with her. He was right. The Beaumonts were freaking amazing and she was proud to be a part of the clan.

"I'm sure your family is something special as well," she managed between sips from her flute. "Tell me about your mother."

There was no mistaking the pride on his face at the mention of his mother. "Lorraine is a force to be reckoned with. She don't take no mess."

Sedona smiled. "She sounds like my mother."

"Yeah she is something else, but all of the Carlson women are. My Aunt Kim is a Philadelphia police officer."

Her brow rose. "Really?"

He nodded and took a sip before continuing. "Twenty-five years on the force. She's now the captain at her precinct."

"That's awesome! I love to hear about women in powerful places. I would love to interview her for a book I'm supposed to be working on."

"What do you mean supposed to be?"

"I've had a hard time coming up with a topic, but hearing about your aunt has me thinking about writing about women making it in professions that were once male dominated."

"Like Laila Ali's decision to box. I get it." His brow rose with admiration. "Good topic. It's also one conversation—as a man—I know to steer the hell away from."

"Why's that?"

He wanted to groan. There was something about the way Sedona held his gaze, the way she licked her lips so sensual and erotic, unaware the effect she had on him. "Because I think there are some roles that should only be male dominated like there are some things that only a woman should do."

"Such as?"

"The military, infantry battalions. I don't think women need to be out there on the frontline fighting."

Sedona shook her head, but did not look upset. "And there are thousands of women who would disagree."

"Maybe so, but call me old-fashioned. I like my woman to feel safe and protected." He shrugged. "Sue me, but I'm a strong believer that men and women have roles."

She groaned. "Don't tell me you're one of those who likes his woman at home barefoot and pregnant."

"I prefer her bent over the sink wearing a thong," he teased.

He found her biting back a grin. "You're kidding right?"

Keith licked his lips and there was humor burning in his eyes. "Or seeing a woman sitting across the table from me with buffalo sauce on the tip of her nose."

Her lips formed an O as he reached over and rubbed

the pad of his thumb across the tip of her nose then brought the finger to his lips and licked it.

He stared at her and felt his cock swell beneath his zipper. He wanted to hold her in his arms, strip her naked, and carry her up to the bedroom.

Damn, he had it bad.

Smiling, she slipped from the stool and carried the empty bowl of salsa to the sink. "You ready to watch the movie?"

At his silence, Sedona looked over her shoulder and cast her eyes in his direction. Keith was sure she saw the raw need burning in their depths.

"What? Did you have something else in mind?"

His eyes were fixated on hers as he rose from the stool. "I want to make love to you."

She faltered, blinking. "You do?" Her voice was a little more than a breath.

"Do you have any objections to that?" Keith asked as he took a step toward her.

Her mouth opened in surprise before she whispered, "I..." Sedona paused and laughed nervously. "I don't know what to say."

"You can say no."

She was fidgeting with the flute in her hand, while her mouth was working as if she had something she wanted to confess. "No, then I would be lying to myself."

His pulse quickened as he took another step toward her. "Then say yes."

She dropped her head momentarily, cheeks flushed with warm color. "I've never had a man ask permission."

"I've never believed in taking anything that wasn't given to me." Keith came to a stop directly in front of her, then took the wine glass from her hand and set it on the counter. "Now answer the question? Can I make love to you?"

Sedona stared up at him, her dark eyes shining, her lips parted. He turned her on. He could hear it in her voice. Saw it in the tension of her body.

"I'd like that very much," she said on a breathy whisper.

"Say yes, Sedona."

Keith backed her up against the dishwasher, and braced his hands on the quartz countertop at both sides of her waist.

"Yes," she conceded.

"Thank you," he told her and leaned in, covering her mouth with his own.

Once again, her lips were warm, wet and addictive, sparking his arousal even higher. The feel of her in his arms was even more unforgettable. Sedona tasted like sweet wine and when he slipped his tongue inside and met hers, she might as well have touched him with a live wire. His body heated and his hands were everywhere, stroking along her ass and thighs then up and cupping the swell of her breasts. She felt so good, and yet nothing he did was enough to simmer the need raging inside him.

Sedona brought her arms up around his neck, dragging him even deeper into the kiss and he deepened it while his fingers continued to explore. Keith brought his hand down to scrub across the crotch of her leggings, and found her warm and aroused. When she whimpered against his lips with need, he knew exactly how the evening was going to end; Sedona's long legs wrapped high around his waist.

She had no idea how badly he wanted to carry her upstairs, tossing her onto the bed, getting her naked and filling his hands and mouth with the rich, sinful taste of her body.

"Your nipples are hard," he told her.

She moaned when he brought his fingers up and rubbed the pad of his calloused thumb across her breast.

"You like that?" Keith managed as he lifted his mouth to catch his breath.

"Mmmm-hmmm," she moaned, and clung to him as he slid his hands down her back and along the sides of her breasts, teasing, wanting.

Her body flinched and the gasps coming from her throat while he trailed his tongue along her slender neck was enough to let him know she was just as aroused as he was. And he was just getting started.

Keith had no intention of stopping until he had satisfied both of their desires. He needed her as desperately as he needed his next breath. It no longer mattered how stupid this move was, that there would be no turning back once he made love to her. Hell, he didn't want to think. Only feel. Sedona had gotten under his skin.

Her mouth opened on a sigh of pleasure when he slid his other hand under her sweater.

While his fingers explored, Keith pulled back slightly to find her eyes were closed, her lips moist and parted. His fingers were firmly planted just below her breast. Squirming, she arched her back.

"What are you waiting for?" she hissed impatiently.

He smirked at the urgency in her voice. "Mother, may I?" he teased.

"Yes," she whispered. "Please touch me now!"

She was clutching onto him now while his fingers squeezed and released her breasts. Panting, Sedona reached up and frantically dragged the sweater over her head, then reached behind and unhooked the clasps to her bra. His eyes were immediately drawn to her breasts.

"You are so fucking beautiful." Perfect size. Shape. And perky. The hardened nipples gave him the sudden urge to suck on a piece of chocolate. Bracing her against the cabinet Keith lowered his mouth to her breast. Her skin was flush with heat and her nipple ripe and ready for his attention. He slipped it between his lips, drawing a pleasurable moan from her that caused his cock to buck against her thigh.

"That feels amazing," she purred.

"Tonight is all about making you feel good." Keith moved his hand around teasing her abdomen, making her muscles pull tight in reaction before dipping under the waistband of her leggings, smoothing his palm over the curve of her ass, then slowly around to caress her inner thighs. Sedona swayed slightly, then tightened her hold on his waist while mumbling something under her breath that he couldn't decipher, but there was no need. Her body spoke volumes.

His tongue had slid to the other breast and he increased the intensity while he smoothed the palm of his hand down across her kitty.

"Keith," she whimpered, causing him to smile against her flesh. Her heart was pounding, breath coming out in small gasps as if desperately trying to squeeze more oxygen into her lungs, and she was wet and creamy right beneath his fingers.

"Babe, slide your pants down for me," he insisted.

Shaky hands came up and dragged the material down lower over her hips, practically to her ankles. His eyes were fixed on the patch of hair covering her pussy. It had been trimmed in a perfect V. It was enticing and his penis bucked in agreement.

"Now spread your legs."

Anxious to see just how aroused he had made her, Keith gently grazed a long finger through her folds, parting her slightly and stirred in a circular motion before he slid down and then up along her clit.

"Shit!" she shuddered and Keith had to growl in order to hold it together. He stared at her, Sedona's eyes smoldering while his fingers gently stroked, easing in slowly before he sank one finger deep inside her.

Sedona moaned and leaned her head back.

Keith stalled. "Open your eyes, babe. I want you to look at me."

She panted, then her bottom lip caught between her teeth before she met his gaze.

"You're already wet." He stared down at the desire in her eyes, and smiled. "How do my fingers make you feel?" He pushed, then withdrew and pushed again. Sedona whimpered. "Feels good?"

"Yes." She rocked her hips against him and groaned.

"How about now?" He pushed a second finger inside her.

"Oh yes," she whispered and her eyelids fluttered close as she panted, "That...feels...amazing."

"Keep your eyes open, Sedona. I want to watch. I want to see how I make you feel." He pulled his fingers out, slowly eased in, out, back in, and he watched the way her breasts rose and her breath hitched. Through a half-lidded gaze she stared at his hand between her thighs.

"You like that?"

"Do you have to ask?" she moaned.

"Actually I do. I want to hear you tell me you like the way my fingers feel inside of your pussy."

Groaning, Sedona managed, "I love the way your...your fingers feel inside me."

She was aroused and that was a total turn-on for him. Dipping his head, Keith captured her nipple, sucking hard.

He brought his thumb up to explore; her clit was swollen, and pulsating. Each stroke of his finger, left her pulsing and panting, and caused his cock to throb with need.

"I want to see your face when you come."

She gasped, eyelids wide.

With a wicked smile, he lowered onto his knees, then pushed apart her inner thighs, making room for his invasion. One finger, then two, he thrust inside of her, then he stroked hard, pretending it was his cock pumping away at her hot center. The desire to be buried inside of her, rushed over him, but he wasn't a greedy or selfish man. There would be plenty of time, he was confident of that. Right now, he was all about pleasing her. With one long stroke, he grazed his thumb across her clit, then added additional pressure. Sedona bucked against the length of his fingers a few times, then tensed, and he watched the pleasure spring upon her face as she neared release.

"That's it."

Sedona whimpered, lips parting, pelvis arching into his palm. Her hips began to pump rapidly in a frantic rhythm against his hand, desperate to take everything his fingers could offer.

"That's it babe…Let it go. Come for me."

And finally her body exploded with the force of a bomb.

◆ ◆ ◆

As her breathing began to slow, Sedona watched

Keith rise to his feet, his eyes were staring hungrily down at her breasts, specifically her nipples, which were hard, raw and yearning for more attention.

Clearing her throat, she managed between pants, "I see you've got skills. That was better than watching a box office movie."

Keith chuckled and kissed her temple. "Babe, that was just the previews. The main attraction is about to begin." He lifted her off the ground and carried her over to the island and propped her on top. Quickly, he gathered all the food and carried it over to the stove out of his way. As he returned, Sedona noticed the hunger blazing in his eyes. And she knew they were definitely not going to be watching a movie tonight, instead they were making their own.

"Time for these to come off." He reached down and dragged her leggings down over her ankles. "You're even more beautiful than I imagined." His eyes burned with approval.

Keith pulled a stool over and sat down in front of her. "Now, where were we? Aaaah, yes, the main attraction." Reaching up, he covered her breasts with his hands as he murmured, "Damn, I love these."

On contact, Sedona jerked and would have possibly slid right off the island except Keith was sitting right between her dangling legs, keeping her in place.

His fingers kneaded and caressed, then tweaked her nipples and it felt so good, she slumped back on the island using her elbows to support her weight. She enjoyed the feeling of being touched by him.

He rose and then his mouth replaced his hands. She breathed in nice and slowly, shuddering as his lips closed around her stiffened nipple.

"Hmmm." She arched her back, offering herself to

him, then groaned, "You're so wrong for this."

"I know," he whispered as his lips nibbled and teased. "But unfortunately I'm not in control of what's happening here."

She stared at him, suckling hungrily at her nipple. "What do you mean, you're not in control?"

Keith paused, and turned dark eyes on her, staring intently. "It's crazy because I can't really explain it, but I've never felt the need to be with someone the way I feel with you," he confessed. "When I'm around you I feel reckless and out of control."

"Oh." She knew exactly how he felt. Ever since she'd first seen his photographs she had been feeling the same way. "I totally understand."

Keith nipped with his teeth, he sucked her nipple softly between his lips again, and she sighed. His tongue twirled around her areola causing her to heat between her thighs, reminding her of another place his lips and tongue had been. "Keith?"

He switched to the other breast, and teased with his tongue. "Hmmm?"

"Let's go to my bedroom."

His head lifted. His eyes were dark and intense. His breathing heavy. "Hell yeah, let's go."

He put his arms around her waist, lifting her up, and Sedona brought her legs around his waist as he carried her through the house. Her body buzzed with anticipation.

"You know I'm about to get in them draws, right?"

Hands braced at his shoulders, she laughed. "What draws? You've already taken them off."

"Oh yeah, that's right." Keith gave a hearty chuckle, as he hurried up the stairs, down the hall to her room, and dumped her laughing onto the bed. Keith immediately followed her down, then leaned forward and touched his mouth to hers with a tender — almost loving — kiss not sexual, but powerful and filled with emotions.

Between soft small kisses to her lips, and cheeks, Keith whispered, "You're so beautiful. I really enjoy being with you."

"So do I," she confessed. "What's happening between us is scary, but I trust you." Cupping his face, she stared up at him. "I want you to make love to me." Her fingers slid across his head, stroked at his cheeks, savoring the feel of his lean jaws.

Keith looked far too serious.

"Sedona, I need to —"

"Shhh." She leaned up and took his mouth, loving his taste. "I want you. And you want me."

"You know I do."

"Good," she cooed. "Then what's stopping you?"

Keith leaned over and captured her lips in another kiss. Only this time it was deeper and much more intimate than before. Things between them were changing — intensifying — but she didn't have long to explore the possibilities when she felt his fingers sliding across her mound.

Sedona loved when he touched her. Everything about him was powerful, alluring and downright addictive. His body was pressed up alongside her and the scent of him filled her mind.

Finally Keith rose and dragged his shirt over his head. Sedona stared up at amazing pecs, a well-defined abdomen, all the wide, hard muscles that surrounded them, and his name and the wings of a falcon tattooed across his chest. He was so freaking sexy.

Keith dropped to his knees onto the carpet, and

dragged Sedona down toward the edge of the bed.

She felt his breath on her skin, "Keith?" she said and quivered.

His lips moved along her inner thighs. "You smell so damn good," he moaned and then his hands were on her upper thighs, spreading her legs wide.

Shock kept her immobilized. "Keith."

"I need to taste you again." He started licking at her inner thighs, easing them further apart. "And I want you to watch me again."

She propped herself up on the bed and stared down at him, his eyes half closed and his lips parted. Damn the sight was a turn-on! When he finally slipped his tongue between her folds, she let out a long breath. In no time Sedona was rocking her hips, meeting the delicious assault of his mouth. Keith took his sweet time, fucking her with his tongue, driving her insane.

"I could lick you all night."

She didn't think she could bear it a moment longer.

"Talk to me, babe. I want to know what you're thinking." He brought his lips up to suck at her clit, then stroked his tongue repeatedly over the quivering flesh.

She somehow managed to say, "I'm thinking…about…how good you are…at that."

"And this?" He pushed his tongue out and in between her swollen lips in short, quick strokes. Burning need began to build again, starting at her breasts, then traveling down toward the source of heat at the center between her legs. Her heart was pounding, lungs were tight, and with need radiating through her body, she wasn't sure how much more she was going to be able to take.

Sedona gasped, "Yes!" She twisted her hips and was seconds away from losing her mind again. His tongue was licking her clit, his hands touching her in all of the right places.

"Keith," she whimpered. While his tongue stroked her spot, she wiggled on the bed. His lips then sucked vigorously, her hips lifting and twisting against his mouth. Sedona gripped the sheets tight as pleasure roared through her body. His hands and his mouth on her were too much.

"Yes, yes!" she cried out. Again, the climax took her so fast it startled her. Her entire body went taut and then she was shaking uncontrollably,

As her breathing slowed, she looked at him, his eyes filled with desire.

"Now," she whimpered between breaths. "I need you inside of me." She wanted it all, the feel of his body against hers, and the pounding of his penis inside of her.

Keith rose. His gaze was attentive and possessive as he unfastened his jeans, kicked off his shoes, and lowered them over his hips. His legs were toned and muscular. Goodness, he had to work out daily. Her eyes traveled down to his gorgeous penis, long and thick, the head beautifully dark. As she stared, she struggled to breathe. Sedona knew he was blessed but she had not at all been prepared for the sight of it up close and personal. He reached down for his wallet, pulled out a condom, tore it open, then rolled it onto the length of his cock.

Keith climbed on top of her, and Sedona's body sizzled at the feel of his warm muscular body between her thighs. *Oh my*, she couldn't remember the last time she had wanted something as badly as she wanted him. His cock pushed against her folds and she thought she was about to go insane. She moaned and writhed, then looked up at him, staring at her with lust-filled eyes.

"You ready for me?"

"Uh-huh," she moaned impatiently.

Keith eased the crown of his cock into her, paused and swore low under his breath. As she drew a breath, he lunged the full length of his erection into her, again and again. Each thrust was so hard and strong it sent her crying out in ecstasy. Keith had her so hot and aroused that every time his cock thrust, a sob ripped from her lips. His strokes were deep and confident and she wrapped her legs around his hips, drawing his penis even deeper. He gripped her hips and pumped vigorously until she thought she was going to pass out from the intense pleasure.

"Oh, it's good!" she cried out as he stroked in and out. "It's so good!"

She was melting and moaning with pleasure. The man was amazing and mind-boggling and a whole lot of other adjectives. The list was becoming endless. It had been so long since she'd made love and it had definitely been worth the wait.

Keith moved faster, long confident strokes that pushed her higher and higher. He continued to pound her with his cock and she was powerless to do anything but enjoy it. His mouth opened and each hard pump drew a harsh breath from between his lips. Keith gathered her in his arms, held her tight as he sank into her again and again. Sedona clawed at his back as heat swelled up inside her until finally she stiffened and another orgasm crashed hard over her. "Keith!"

"That's it baby...let it go," Keith urged as the walls of her vagina tightened around him. And then just as she peaked, she felt his body become taut and a long roar ripped from between his lips followed by the quiver of three hard jerks of his hips.

Moments later Sedona was lying limp on her back,

gasping for air while he lied beside her, stroking her from shoulder to hip before collecting her carefully in his arms.

"I advise you to get some rest. We're just getting started," Keith whispered, then lowered his mouth over her lips in a kiss strong enough to melt her into submission all over again. Turning onto her side, she cuddled in his arms while her mind began to spin at the possibility.

Keith was right. They were in for a long night.

Chapter 9

Keith woke to discover he wasn't in bed alone, and a beautiful woman was curled beside him. He did a full-body stretch as the memories came rushing back. And he summed it up in one word.

Sensational.

He'd been at Sedona's house, in her room, sharing her bed for the last two incredibly sex-filled nights, and he couldn't get enough of her. If it had been any other woman, Keith would have left long before the sun had risen, but with Sedona he had no desire to distance himself from her.

Keith shifted his head to the left and gazed at her beautiful face. A pillow cushioned her head. She was in a deep sleep and snoring so softly that he actually found the sound sexy. She was lying face down, head turned, and the magnolia tattoo on her left shoulder was staring at him. The room was warm and comfortable, yet Sedona had kicked the blanket away. He followed the length of her back across smooth skin down to the dip just above the swell of her perfectly-toned ass. Admiring her and all her lush curves had him thinking about some of the wicked things they had done. The last round of mind-boggling sex had been less than four hours ago. He should be exhausted, instead he already wanted to be inside her again.

He blew out a long breath, slid out from underneath

the blanket, then covered her body to her shoulders. Reaching down for his boxers, he slipped his legs inside, then pulled them up on his waist as he left the room.

While he walked downstairs and through her house, he admired the décor. Her space was warm, inviting and definitely had a woman's touch. Nothing like his place. This wasn't just a house. It was a home.

He went down to the kitchen. The tiles felt cool beneath his bare feet. A glass was sitting in the rack on the sink. Keith reached for it, walked to the fridge and filled it with the automatic ice cubes and water then brought the glass to his lips and took a long thirsty swallow. He felt dehydrated, drained and desperate for something to cool his loins and the sudden insatiable appetite he had for Sedona.

The sex, the time they had spent together talking and sharing, it had been magical. He loved everything about her. She was smart and funny with a dry humor he adored. She was beautiful and sexy and did things with her eyes she probably wasn't even aware of doing. There was no denying the two of them had a connection that was like nothing he'd experienced with another woman. With Sedona he felt alive in a weird way. She made him want to share parts of his life he rarely talked about. But as Keith took a thirsty swallow, a nagging thought filtered through his mind that caused him to lower the glass to the counter with a bang.

He still hadn't told her the truth. A ball of regret settled at his stomach.

Pushing away from the sink, Keith walked across the kitchen floor, took a seat at the table in the breakfast nook and stared out into the lush green yard as he tried to sort out his thoughts. He'd had every opportunity to come clean and tell Sedona the truth only he hadn't. *Why is that?* he asked although he already knew. He liked her. He liked her a lot and that was the problem. Maybe if he had said something before they had sex, but now. After making love to her...sharing her bed for the last two days, Sedona was going to feel betrayed and deceived, and she had every right.

Keith dragged a frustrated hand across his head. He was in way over his head and wasn't sure how he could fix it except by telling her the truth. He also knew once he did...what they had...what they shared...would possibly be over.

Angrily, he pushed from the chair almost sending it tumbling back and paced the length of the kitchen as he tried to think of the right approach. Definitely not like this in his boxers and her lying naked in bed. There was no way he could tell her now. He would have to wait and tell her when they were both fully dressed and out of the kitchen — away from the knives.

With a heavy sigh, he wandered through the house into a formal living room, over to a wall of black sculptures. As his eyes perused the shelf, he stalled when they landed on a photograph of Webb. He reached for the frame and stared at the two. Webb was in his service dress uniform and Sedona was wearing a long, blue, ballroom gown. His stomach did a flip-flop. She was young and beautiful. The couple looked perfectly happy and ready to share a future.

A future he'd once envied and now craved for himself.

"What are you doing up?"

Keith startled when Sedona sneaked up behind him, and wrapped her slender arms around his waist. "The bed was lonely without you," she purred softly.

"I couldn't sleep and didn't want to disturb you." He

put the photograph back on the shelf but not before Sedona noticed.

"I was only twenty-one. Webb had just been promoted to a petty officer and that was our first formal event." She released her hold around his waist, leaned forward and reached for the photograph. Sedona stared down at it with a smile curling her lips slightly upward. She looked so innocent. Her hair was rumpled and she had a soft, sleepy look on her face.

"It looks like the two of you were happy," he heard himself say.

She nodded and didn't bother to look up as she said softly, "We were very happy. Full of hopes and dreams. I was going to finish college, then we were supposed to marry and start a family." Sedona sighed and placed the frame back onto the shelf. "I always wanted a big family like my parents. Not exactly seven children, but Webb was an only child so he always said the more the merrier." She shrugged, then met Keith's eyes. He studied her. Sedona looked so fragile. Her gaze was warm, sad, and intense. "I didn't think I'd ever find the strength to move on with my life."

Keith was practically holding his breath while he searched her face for answers. "And have you?"

She nodded. "Yes. He will always have a special place in my heart, but I know he would have wanted me to get on with my life and find happiness."

Possessiveness clutched at his chest as he reached up and caressed the side of her face, allowing his long fingers to peruse the smooth skin at her chin and neck. "I bet he's smiling at you right now."

"I sure hope so." Sedona gave him a crooked smile. "You know what? I think he would have really liked you." Rising upon her toes, she pressed her soft, warm lips against his, then scampered into the kitchen, leaving Keith standing there stunned and feeling more like he'd betrayed her than before.

Chapter 10

"Who it this guy I overheard Aunt Jessica talking to Mom about?"

Sedona didn't dare look in Sage's direction as she sauntered across the department store's gleaming white floor. "What are you talking about?" Sedona replied as she played dumb.

Her younger sister blew out a slow breath. "You know what I'm talking about. Bianca said you met some freak online."

Her head whipped to her left. "Freak? She called Keith a freak?"

Sage chuckled. "No, I added that part. So his name's Keith?"

"You're too much." Sedona rolled her eyes and headed over to the perfume counter.

"When did you decide to meet a man online?"

Sedona brought a small pink glass bottle to her nose and sniffed. "It was Bianca's, idea but how else would I meet a man? I don't do the club scene or hang out at car shows like you."

Sage scrunched up her small nose. "But internet dating? The men online, they are all desperate and weird."

"Not all of them," Sedona replied and then smirked as she moved around the counter with her sister's thigh-high chocolate boots clicking on the floor with each step.

"So you're saying this Keith guy isn't homely?"

She stared at Sage for a moment then let loose a long-suffering sigh, deciding any attempt to hide her feelings from her sister would be a big waste of time. "Nope. The complete opposite."

Sage quirked a perfectly arched eyebrow in disbelief. "Then something must be wrong with him."

"Then that means something has to be wrong with me too, because my profile was also on that site," she pointed out with a hard stare.

"Okay, you got me there," she said holding a hand up in surrender.

With a grin Sedona sprayed a purple perfume bottle at her wrist. "Mmmm. I like this one." She held out her wrist and Sage took a sniff.

"That is nice," she agreed.

"I think Mom will love it." She signaled for the sales associate. "Can I get the gift set please?"

As soon as the fifty-something woman nodded and went off to ring up the order, Sage started in again. "Let's get back to this Keith guy...what's his story?"

"Why does he have to have a story? He's—" Sedona broke off when she noticed a tall dark-skinned guy walking past the counter staring at her sister's ass. "You got an audience," she teased under her breath.

Sage took one bold look then rolled her eyes dramatically toward the ceiling. "Ugh, his jeans are too tight."

Sedona exploded with laughter. "No, they are not."

She gave a dismissive wave of her hand. "Quit changing the subject, Donie."

"Okay, hold on a moment." She handed her credit card to the salesclerk, then turned and faced her sister. "He's retired Navy."

Sage's eyes narrowed and she could see the concern.

"Another Navy man? How do you feel about that?"

Sedona retrieved her credit card and returned it to her wallet as she replied, "I live in Hampton Roads. The majority of men in the area work at the shipyards, are active duty or have already retired."

Sage nodded and waited for her to sign the receipt and get her bag before she fell into step beside Sedona. They exited the department store and headed out into the mall.

"So do you like him?"

She couldn't resist a smile and glanced over her shoulder and admitted, "Yeah, I like him a lot."

"Awww get it! Get it!" Sage screamed, then leaned over and playfully bumped her sister's shoulder causing her to giggle again. "Maybe this dude is the real thing because I can't remember the last time I heard you laugh like this."

A grin was curling her painted lips as she looked over at Sage without breaking stride. "With a man like him in my life you can't do anything but smile."

Sage suddenly stopped. Sedona also stalled, turned and looked at her. "What's wrong?"

"Nothing," Sage said and resumed walking. "I'm just surprised. I haven't heard you talk about a man since… since Derrick."

Sedona momentarily stared straight ahead as she proceeded through the mall. "I haven't had a man worth talking about…then again, maybe I just wasn't ready."

Sage curled an arm across her sister's shoulders. "Or maybe you were waiting to meet Keith."

She turned and the sisters grinned foolishly at each other. Just the thought of the gorgeous man made her heart flutter.

"Are you planning on bringing him home for

Christmas?"

There was a pregnant pause before she replied, "I don't know. I haven't thought past this week."

Sage's voice was teasing when she said, "Probably a good thing. He might not be ready to meet the Force MDs."

"I think you might be wrong." And following a laugh, Sedona dragged her sister into the lingerie store.

♦ ♦ ♦

"Who the hell moves in December?" Keith said under his breath while he carried the large cardboard box up the flight of stairs and lowered it at the center of the apartment floor. "Mason, man, that's the last box."

The short stocky man dropped three smaller boxes to the far wall of the crowded space, then turned and walked over to grab the final addition. "Falcon, good looking out."

Keith gave him a fist bump then nodded. "No problem."

The two had served in Korea together. Mason had returned to the Virginia Beach area and was now working as a contractor for the Coast Guard.

"Would you like something to eat?"

At the sound of the sweet feminine voice, Keith looked over at Kimmie, Mason's fiancée, standing near the door of the living room. "I can whip up some cheeseburgers," she added and pushed a lock of auburn hair away from her mocha-colored forehead.

Keith nodded. He hadn't eaten since lunch time and it was already after five. "A burger sounds great."

"Sweetheart, make that two." Mason smiled over at the woman he had confessed to being the love of his life.

Keith watched as the two embraced and then kissed, momentarily forgetting he was even in the room. He gave a playful groan. The two had been at it all afternoon. Turning on the balls of his feet, he made his way over to the large picturesque window and stared out at the parking lot below.

His cell phone chirped and he reached inside the pocket of his leather jacket, thankful for the distraction. As soon as he identified Sedona's number on the screen, his lips curled upward with pleasure.

"Hey you," he greeted.

"Hi," she said in that soft voice that did wicked things to his libido. "What are you doing?"

"Just finishing up helping one of my boys move," he replied as he headed from the living room toward the hall for a little privacy.

"Sounds exhausting. I just spent the last five hours fighting crowds, Christmas shopping with my sister."

"Now that sounds exhausting," he said in mock disgust.

Sedona chuckled heartily and he marveled at the musical sounds.

"Well," she began, "I was calling because I was hoping you could take me to get a Christmas tree."

"A Christmas tree?" he sputtered with amusement.

"Yes," she purred in his ear. "You think you have time?"

"Babe, for you I'll make time. Let me run home and clean up and then I'll come pick you up." Keith headed back toward the living room.

"Sounds like a plan."

He was still grinning long after he ended the call. When he stepped into the room, the couple was staring at him.

"I guess you won't be staying for dinner?" Mason asked inquisitively.

There was humor twitching in Kimmie's eyes.

He shook his head. "No bruh, I definitely will not."

Chapter 11

"I like that one over there."

Keith watched with amusement while Sedona sauntered over to another Christmas tree and examined it. They had been at it for almost an hour and she still hadn't made a decision.

"I think this might be the one."

Keith chuckled. "You said the same thing about the last five."

Sedona turned her head and gave him an innocent look that made his heart practically leap from his chest.

He'd spent his entire life thinking selecting a Christmas tree was quick and easy, but Sedona had brought on an entirely different perspective. Instead of picking out a tree in front of the grocery store, she instructed him to take her to a nursery not far from Langley Air Force Base where there were hundreds of Douglas firs. He watched and listened with fascination as she gave him the history of the tree as she walked down one row after another in search of the perfect one.

"What do you think?" she asked, and glanced over her shoulder to meet his gaze.

Falcon made a show of examining it. The tree was thick and the limbs nice and green. And it looked exactly like the last half dozen they'd seen.

"I think it's a perfect choice," he agreed.

"Hmmm," Sedona replied doubtfully and no longer looked convinced.

It took everything not to laugh when she walked off and started searching trees again.

With his hands tucked in the pockets of a leather bomber jacket, he watched the magical sway of her hips in blue jeans. Keith shook his head with appreciation. She definitely had one amazing ass. While she'd been conducting her search, he'd been taking advantage of the opportunity to appreciate all of her fine qualities and lush curves that he was dying to hold in his hands again. Sedona was wearing leather riding boots that traveled up her long slender legs and a wool pea coat that accented her narrow waist.

Tonight was the first night he had seen her since their two-day sex marathon and tonight, when the moment was right, they were going to have a long talk. Guilt was nagging away at his insides and had lain heavily on his mind all day at work. The sooner he told her the truth the better. He would just have to accept the consequences no matter what they might be.

"Thanks for all your help," Sedona said. Keith blinked and realized she was standing right in front of him.

"Have you decided on a tree?" Reaching out, he snaked an arm around her middle. Damn, he couldn't keep his hands to himself.

Tilting her head, Sedona said with a smile, "I decided to go with the last choice."

"Good decision."

She was grinning. "I bet you didn't think I'd ever make a decision."

"You could say that," Keith replied and chuckled.

"You should try shopping for Christmas presents with me," she replied and winked before she walked off to find the attendant.

Once the tree was paid for, Keith insisted that Sedona climb into the vehicle with the seat-warmers on while he strapped it to the roof of an old GMC Jimmy he kept around just for moments like these.

When he finally climbed inside out of the cold, Sedona screeched, "That was fun!" She was smiling over at him. *God, her dark eyes were gorgeous.* Better yet was what he could see radiating through them — inner beauty, laughter and desire.

He nodded. "That *was* quite interesting."

As he pulled down the street, she stared out the window, at the Christmas lights blinking from a storefront window directly across the street, before swiveling to him to say, "You've never shopped for a tree before, have you?"

Keith took his eyes off the road long enough to give her a look. "How'd you guess?"

"It wasn't that hard."

He shrugged as he made a right onto Armistead Road. "I never had to."

"What about growing up?"

"Dad used to just bring a tree to the house. We were so excited we never questioned where he got it."

"Picking out the tree is my favorite part," Sedona explained. "When I was growing up, Christmas was always a special time around our house. For instance, the morning after Thanksgiving, we'd all get up, have breakfast, then head to the nursery to pick out a tree. It took us hours to find just the right one."

"Hours? Really? I would have never guessed that."

Sedona smirked. "I got myself a jokester."

Keith roared with laughter. "Laughter is how I managed to stay looking so young."

Sedona chuckled along with him and once again the

sound did crazy things to the pit of his stomach. Once she sobered she said, "Was the tree decorating a family event in your house?"

He didn't bother to look her way while he shook his head. "Nope. My brother and I decorated the tree any way we wanted. Trust me. Some years that was one sad tree. We'd string popcorn and eat half of it before we got it on the tree," he paused and laughed. "We also had homemade decorations and Mom made some at her dress shop." He stopped at a red light and fixed his eyes on her. "Let me guess? Your tree had crystal balls and hundreds of beautiful decorative ornaments."

She shook her head. "Not at all. We have a lot of unique Christmas ornaments that have been in my mother's family for generations, but the rest are individual items we have either created or contributed."

"What do you mean, contributed?"

As he continued down the road, Sedona turned slightly on the seat as she continued, "Each piece has to tell a story. For instance...my brother Remy was in Belize and he bought an ornament from a little boy, a street vendor who lost his legs in a car accident. The Christmas bells were carved from tree bark and stained red from berries."

He whistled. "Wow! Is this a tradition?"

Sedona nodded and he could see the pride in her eyes. "Christmas is a time for being thankful and my brothers and I believe in family and traditions."

"I'm sure you've started a tradition of your own."

She gave a tell-all smile. "If you mean if I've been collecting unique items to decorate my tree, I just started so this tree will have more store-brought ornaments than anything else. However, I've been slowly building my own story. I hope the tradition will continue when I have a family of my own."

He smiled. Sedona was definitely an amazing woman and the more time they spent together the more he understood why Webb had loved her so much. "You are an interesting woman, Sedona Beaumont."

He loved the way she tucked her chin and blushed before she replied, "Thank you."

They were quiet the rest of the ride to her house. Keith took the time to think about the upcoming holiday and the likelihood of sharing part of it together. He sure hoped so. He could already visualize Sedona's eyes wide with excitement as he handed her a Christmas present. The big question would be, what would he give her? Especially for a woman who appeared to already have everything.

Keith pulled up the long driveway, turned off the SUV, then hurried around and opened the door for her, and together they unstrapped the tree. Sedona unlocked the double doors while Keith carried the fir inside.

"Bring it in here," she instructed and he stepped in the spacious living room. "Put it in the corner near the window. The stand has already been set up."

He carried it over, but with the size of the tree he could barely see where he was going and bumped into the coffee table.

"What do you need me to do?" Sedona asked as she unzipped her coat and tossed it onto a cream colored sofa.

"If you could guide the base of the tree into the stand that would be great."

"Gotcha." She lowered to her knees and crawled over to the corner. When she looked up at him innocently with those doe-shaped eyes, it took effort to get his body not to react to her being in his favorite position — doggy-style. Unfortunately his mind wandered somewhere it had no business going which included her unsnapping his jeans, lowering the zipper then reaching inside for his —.

Keith cleared his throat and pushed the thought aside. He raised the tree over the stand and with Sedona's assistance lowered it into place. She tightened the tree and then he stepped back as she rose and stood beside him.

"Looks perfect," she murmured and the sound did something to his insides.

"Yes it is." Only he wasn't talking about the tree. He was referring to the beautiful woman standing beside him. He brought a hand up and cupped her shoulder and tried to ignore how comfortable he felt around her.

◆ ◆ ◆

"If you aren't in a rush to go, take off your coat and stay awhile," Sedona said, then eased away from his arousing touch and over to flick the switch to light the gas fireplace. While she knelt down and waited for the pilot to light, she noticed her hands were shaking and it had nothing to do with the cold outside. Keith's long, strong fingers had her body on high alert. What was happening to her? She had been aroused from the moment he had arrived at her house to take her tree shopping. Just the sight of the tall gorgeous man sitting behind the wheel was enough to make her blood sizzle. He had her so off balance she had a hard time thinking, which made finding the perfect tree twice as difficult. Keith's genuine interest in her family's Christmas traditions only heightened her attraction to him.

Once the fire was lit, she rose to her feet. "Would you

like something to drink?"

"Some water will be great." He was looking down at the crates beside the sofa. "Are these your decorations?"

She nodded. "Yes they are. Let me get you some water." She turned on the balls of her feet and headed toward the kitchen as she said, "I was planning to decorate the house this evening. You're more than welcome to help if you want."

"I'd love to."

I was hoping you would say that, she thought with a shiver and hurried off to grab two bottles of water. Once in the kitchen, Sedona leaned her forehead against the stainless steel refrigerator and drew a breath. Keith had done all kinds of naughty things to her in this room and already her clit was pulsing and yearning for an encore.

Get it together, Donie.

As much as her nipples throbbed in remembrance, the last thing she wanted was to find herself in a sexual relationship, not that she had any complaints in that area. Keith was truly a beast in bed. However, she wanted a relationship that had a stronger foundation than just sex. She just hoped Keith wanted the same.

A moment later, Sedona walked back into the living room. "Here you go."

"Thanks." Keith took the bottle from her, unscrewed the cap, then pointed to the hardwood floor. "I started untangling your lights and testing them. That's the only one that doesn't work."

Her gaze shifted to the string of multicolored lights. "There's probably a bad bulb that needs replacing. I should have some bulbs in the box."

"Gotcha." He took a long thirsty swallow, then rummaged through the decorations. Sedona moved to her iPod on the docking station and clicked on the music.

Donnie Hathaway was singing, "This Christmas".

Keith shook his head and smiled up from the floor where he was kneeling. "Nothing gets you in the holiday spirit like Christmas music."

She smiled in agreement. "Some of the stations are now playing nonstop Christmas music until New Year's. A lot of throwbacks, but it's great." She slapped her hands together. "Okay, so let's get started. Since you offered, I plan on using your muscles."

"Muscles? What do you have in mind?" Keith licked his lips and gave her a look that almost made Sedona question her decision to behave.

"I have some reindeer in the garage. I would love for you to carry them out to the front yard."

"Sure thing." He took another long drink from the bottle, then returned the cap. "Lead the way."

Sedona signaled for him to follow her through the house and could feel the heat of his gaze watching the sway of her ass. She was glad she decided to wear her favorite jeans.

As they walked through the kitchen, Cocoa scurried across the room over to her milk dish. She smiled and continued out the side door into the garage and hit the switch.

Keith whistled. "This is the cleanest garage I've ever seen."

She smiled, "Probably because I rarely use it."

Sedona pointed to a large box to the far side of the space. "The reindeer are over there." She walked past him. Boxes were neatly lined along the wall. There were also metal shelves. Everything was labeled and organized. She saw the way Keith was looking at her and started laughing.

"Okay, so this might be a little too organized. To tell

you the truth, I did a webinar on decluttering your life which includes your personal life. I found an online company that comes out, assesses the space, and then recommends ways to fully utilize the area. They had my garage fully functional in no time."

He had an amused look on his face. "You're definitely a piece of work."

"Yes, I guess you could say that." She gave a nervous laugh and decided to stay focused on the reindeer and not his pretty white teeth. "The deer are overhead." She started to walk past when Keith reached out and caught her around the waist.

"What in the world am I gonna do with you?" he said softly.

"I don't know, but I'm sure you'll think of something."

Keith lowered his mouth to claim hers or maybe she tilted her head; Sedona wasn't quite sure. All she knew was she'd waited all evening for the moment to feel his lips over hers in a kiss that was such a turn-on she had to resist the urge to moan into his mouth.

"I needed to taste you," he whispered a breath away from her lips.

"What took you so long?" she replied, her lips a hair away from his.

He took her mouth again and this time it was far from gentle. In fact it was thorough, confident, like he was staking his claim while at the same time building a fire within her chest. The kiss was hungry like he was a starving man who'd been deprived of what he needed for far too long.

She purred into his mouth as he deepened the kiss and sank his fingers into her hair, holding her in place. His tongue dipped inside and she followed his lead because nothing turned her on more than a man who was in control. Taking what he wanted, teasing, taunting, enticing until their hands were sliding up and down each other's backs. Sedona's fingers were ready to lower his zipper and reach inside when Keith finally ended the kiss.

Reaching up, his fingers stroked the side of her cheek. "I was trying to resist you, but you make it so hard."

"I'm going to take that as a compliment."

"That it is," he agreed and slid one hand behind her neck and tilted her head as he took another long kiss before he finally released her. "Now show me those reindeer before I carry you back inside the house and make love to you," he said, letting his hands drop.

He'd get no complaints from her.

While they decorated the tree, Sedona had a pizza delivered, then together they set up the animals in her front yard. Keith even strung lights around her front door and windows. When it was all done, she made them both a cup of hot chocolate with plenty of marshmallows and they went out and sat in his SUV and watched the lights twinkle. It was her favorite time of the year.

By the time they had gone back into the house Toni Braxton was singing "Silent Night". Sedona hung their coats in the hall closet. Everything looked perfect. Red bows on the uprights of the stairs. Christmas tree decorated with blinking lights.

"What would you like to do now?" Keith asked and reached for her hand drawing Sedona close to him.

Desire bloomed in her stomach. "Maybe relax on the couch and actually watch a movie," she teased.

"I guess we can give it a try." Keith winked.

"That's if I can stop shivering. I think we were outside

a bit too long for my bones." Her teeth were chattering.

He rubbed his hands up and down her arms trying to warm her body. "You're an icebox! Why don't you run upstairs and take a hot shower before the movie?"

Her knees shook. "I got a better idea. How about we go upstairs and take a hot jetted bath together?"

Eyes beaming with hunger, Keith leaned in close and planted a loving kiss to her lips as he said quietly, "Lead the way."

♦ ♦ ♦

"You actually got me feeling the Christmas spirit."

Keith was leaned back in the tub with Sedona sitting between his legs. The water was up to her forearms with bubbles floating around. Her back was pressed up against his chest with his arms around her, making her feel safe and desired. She wasn't sure how long they had been in the water, but it had at least been long enough for the feel of his hot flesh to warm her body.

She closed her eyes and rested her head on his chest. How she loved his strength and raw power. "I love this time of year," she said as she dragged a leg up close to her body.

"I have a feeling this Christmas might end up being my favorite."

Keith lathered the washcloth and in slow movements stroked the cloth across her arms and breasts. As he caressed her nipples, Sedona's breathing became heavy. If he was trying to arouse her, he was doing a pretty good job, and when his hand traveled up her inner thighs, her knees shook with anticipation.

"Are you purposely trying to start something?" she purred.

"Nope," he said, but his erection pressed against her back jutted and said otherwise.

He dropped the cloth and used his bare hands. One hand palmed her breasts into submission. The other slid down past her belly to explore between her thighs and it wasn't long before his long fingers slipped between her folds and explored. Sedona shivered and went limp when his fingers slid in and out of her kitty with such gentle care. She closed her eyes and enjoyed the foreplay, but it wasn't long before she wanted more.

She swung around in the tub, sat back on her heels, and faced him. Keith watched her beneath half-lowered lashes, desire glinting in his eyes. Her gaze wandered down his chest to where his swollen penis was bobbing in and out of the water. *God, he was gorgeous.*

She gave a tiny smile. "Are you ready to get out?"

He shook his head. "No."

"What's on your mind?" she whispered.

"You." His wicked grin confirmed what she was thinking. "What's on *your* mind?"

"You...this." She reached down and stroked his rock hard penis and felt him flinch between her fingers. She cupped her hand around the base, stroking upward in a gentle motion. It was meant to be playful.

His breath caught.

Beneath the water, Sedona gently massaged his balls. She then dropped her head, kissed the tip slowly at first, and then sucked his penis deep inside her mouth.

"Shit." Keith blew out air, slowly, from between his lips.

"Did you say something?" she asked as her tongue snaked around the head.

Keith's body jerked and he made a restrained snarling sound. "Yeah..., don't stop."

Laughing, she swallowed his cock, taking him to the back of her throat, then sucked while stroking her hand up and down his rigid shaft.

"That's it baby, suck that dick... suck it." Moaning, he brought his hands to the top of her head then fisted her hair and started guiding her pumps.

Sedona continued administering what she hoped was the best blow job Keith had ever had. The way his hips were rocking and the tight hold he had on her hair, gave her the assurance she was providing him agonizing pleasure.

"That feels so good, babe." His hips arched to meet her.

She picked up the pace, sliding her lips up and down his length, massaged his balls, then swallowed him even deeper. A loud growl ripped from his throat, then abruptly, he lifted her head, and withdrew his length from her mouth.

"I was just get—"

"Babe, another second and it would have been over. I've got other plans." His words came out breathless, laced with lust. Keith kissed her possessively, pushed his tongue between her lips and explored her mouth, the same place his cock had been only seconds ago. Blood pounded in her ears, shutting out all sounds around them.

He finally drew away leaving her feeling dazed, then grabbed her forearms and lifted her over his body until she was straddling his lap.

"Oh," she whimpered as he gripped her hips and dragged her along the length of his cock.

Suddenly, Keith snapped his fingers. "Oh damn! I forgot the condom," he said and frowned.

"We don't need it. I'm on the pill," Sedona assured

him and before he could react, she slid down over his length. Keith released a long hiss, then gripped her hips again, holding her down against his body.

"Let me ride you," she whispered.

"That's it," Keith growled while thrusting his cock upward, hard and deep. "You feel so good, Sedona."

"Yes!" she cried out and struggled to breathe. How was it her body was starving for something only he could give? As she rocked her hips and met his upward pumps, Keith focused his attention on her nipples, gently licking and kissing first one, then the other, again and again. He was driving her insane.

"Your pussy is so tight," he whispered while rolling his hips, driving himself even deeper.

Holding onto his wide shoulders, she rode him for several long seconds. "Kiss me," she begged.

He dragged her head down and captured her mouth in a deep kiss, making it almost impossible for her to think, only respond. She began winding her hips and moving in small quick strokes and she noticed Keith's breathing had increased.

"Stand up," he growled.

"What?" she asked as she continued to pump her hips.

"Stand up," he ordered and helped Sedona to her feet. "Now turn around and bend over."

As soon as she leaned over, he placed a hand at her back, then moved in close. She felt his cock grazing her ass.

"Look at that sight," she heard him say in a voice that was almost savage. "Put one foot up on the side of the tub."

She did, spreading her thighs, then grabbed onto the towel rack above her head for leverage.

"That's it," Keith coaxed and then he reached down and probed her entrance, preparing her for his penetration.

Sedona was more than ready.

"Put it in," he whispered in her ear.

Reaching behind her, Sedona wrapped her fingers around his erection and positioned it at her entrance. She barely had time to prepare before Keith thrust hard, imbedding himself inside her.

"Ooh!" she whispered.

"You like that?" He didn't even wait for an answer and plunged deeper. "Baby, move with me."

"Yesss..., oh..., yes." She thrust her hips backwards meeting his, pound for pound.

Keith gripped her hips, pumping into her with great speed. Sedona screamed with pleasure. He was large and she felt full. Last time had been amazing, but this time was fucking phenomenal. Her legs grew weak and as he thrust harder and deeper she wondered how long she would be able to hold on.

"I'm about to come," she whimpered as she felt the tension building.

"How about I help you along?" he offered. His hand slipped down across her belly and further still until his fingers brushed over her clit. She whimpered on contact. He circled it, teased it until she shook.

"Keith!"

"Come, babe," he moaned against her ear. "I want to feel you come on my dick."

His strokes grew harder and deeper and Sedona felt like a ship tossed upon a stormy ocean. Keith had the reins. He was in charge. Release was all contingent on the power he had over her mind and body. And she felt ready to explode.

Keith was filling her again and again and the sound of wet flesh smacking a wet ass had her so turned on she felt bombarded with the need for release. Her eyes were closed. Her lips parted and moans were flying from her throat. Each pump, every hard stroke not only drove her arousal up another notch toward release but also heightened her feelings for Keith.

There was much more than just a physical connection going on here. He had aroused not only her body, but her soul as well. Keith wasn't just penetrating her core but also her heart. Emotions were swirling around. She was confused, but too aroused and desperate for release to focus on what was actually happening to her.

He changed the position slightly and started pumping in an uneven circular motion. One hand was at her ass the other found her clit and began manipulating the throbbing bead, causing her to gasp.

"Let it go," he encouraged. And finally she gasped and an orgasm claimed her. Sedona screamed just as Keith growled and started pumping faster and within seconds he shuddered, gave her two final strokes and stilled.

Breathing heavily, she struggled to a standing position while still supporting her weight with the towel rack. Keith leaned in close, his body meshing against hers while he dropped kisses to her cheek.

"Daaayum, babe."

While struggling to catch her breath, she sagged into his arms. "You can say that again."

Laughing, Keith kissed her tenderly on the lips and lifted her into his arms. "Let's take this to bed. " He carried her out the tub and into the bedroom where they both sank under the covers and into each other's arms.

Chapter 12

It was the start of her Dream to Achieve Tour and yet instead of being excited about the enthusiastic crowd of entrepreneurs piling into the large auditorium at the University of Delaware, Sedona caught herself again checking her cell phone for a text message from Keith.

Damn, she had it bad.

Over the last two weeks they had settled into a routine. Almost like a married couple, she thought with a smile, and she was anxious to get back home to him. They weren't actually living together, but that hadn't stopped them from spending all of their free time with each other.

After work Keith usually went home to shower and change, but lately he had been coming straight to her house from the shipyard. He was there at the door ready to drag her into his arms and kiss her.

And on the days she didn't have appointments, Sedona drove to Portsmouth to have lunch with him, and then she was back at home preparing a romantic dinner for his arrival. She loved being with him. Loved that they talked on the phone and texted each other regularly. She especially enjoyed the evenings they spent lounging on the couch, sharing a bowl of popcorn while watching the football game or a movie. Last weekend they spent Sunday watching marathons of *The Walking Dead*.

Yesterday, she'd played hooky. Keith had the day off so Sedona decided to give Energi the day off, and the two stayed in bed feeding their insatiable appetite for each other before the hunger in their stomachs sent them down to the kitchen, where she scrambled eggs while Keith fried bacon.

Hearing voices on the other side of the curtain, Sedona dragged herself away from her thoughts and paced around the narrow space behind the stage. She really needed to stay focused. Today was a milestone for her that she hoped would take her to the next level in her career. Sedona sighed. It was funny how something that was once so important to her had taken a back seat. She was more interested in the future of her relationship with Keith, than she was her new tour, and that scared her. The problem was they hadn't discussed the future. It seemed like they were enjoying the moment and having a good time, but Sedona wanted more. A lot more. She hadn't joined the online site just to find someone to make her smile and to spend time with, not that those things weren't important. She had joined because she wanted to meet a man who she could settle down with and start a future together, and she wanted those things with Keith. But did he want the same? Sedona sighed because in all honesty she wasn't sure. There was no doubt in her mind there wasn't another woman in his life. So what was stopping him from sharing his feelings about their relationship?

The sounds of the MBA program director, Dr. Mary Childress, speaking to the audience drew Sedona from her thoughts, and as soon as she heard her name followed by the introduction there was a round of applause. Sedona drew a deep breath, put on her game face, and sauntered out onto the stage.

"Good morning!"

"Good morning!" The crowd cheered and she smiled as she felt the enthusiasm floating around the room. They had paid good money for her knowledge and she was getting ready to give them their money's worth. She clipped on her microphone and sauntered across the stage as she spoke.

"The dream of the corner office on the penthouse floor has disappeared! POOF! Vanished! Instead, entrepreneurs now aspire to create their own work from home lifestyle, whether that means sitting on a chaise lounge in the sunroom of your home typing a memo, or emailing by a pool at a tropical island resort. My mission today is to show you how to start and grow a business that affords you the freedom to work from home. Entrepreneurship. Freedom. Flexibility. If you can dream it, I can show you what you need to do to achieve it. Ladies and gentlemen… get out your pens and paper and let's begin…"

◆ ◆ ◆

"Oh Debra, these are so good!" It took everything Sedona could do not to moan as she took another bite of the warm sweet taste of her second red velvet cupcake. "Something told me to keep driving and not drop by here."

"I'm glad you did."

They were sitting at a table in the corner of *DebbieCakes* near a large wood-burning fireplace. She took another sip of coffee then bit into the sweet, creamy cheesecake icing. "You're going to bring some of these to my parent's for Christmas, right?"

The voluptuous beauty smiled. "I've already been

instructed to bring several dozen assorted flavors. Your mother actually called my assistant and placed an order just to make sure I had time."

"Good idea. I guess that's what I need to start doing if I want some as well."

Her sister-in-law looked adorable in a blue sweater and black leggings. Usually Debra was behind the counter with flour in her hair, but since she had expanded, she hired enough staff that she was able to work half days leaving her plenty of time to be with the baby. Rance was in Philadelphia practicing for a game scheduled for tomorrow night, and his wife was planning to drive down in the morning and leave Tyrese Christopher with Bianca and London.

"How was the speaking engagement?"

Sedona took a deep breath, and the mostly-heavenly sweet scents filled her nostrils as she spoke. "Phenomenal. My assistant called. I'm scheduled to talk to Steve Harvey after the holidays."

"You're kidding me?" she chirped. Her luminescent skin made her green eyes look wider than usual.

"Would I joke about something like that? According to Energi, Steve is putting together a panel of experts to help entrepreneurs reach their dream of being their own bosses. Somehow he heard about my tour and is interested in possibly adding me to his lineup of speakers."

"Oh, Sedona, that's wonderful." Her thick curly hair bounced with every move.

"I know, right." Her career was booming faster than she had imagined. It seemed that everything in her life—both professional and personal—was coming together. Now if she only knew where Keith's head was in regards to their future.

The silver bell jingled over the door. Sedona watched the flow of customers that were filtering in and out of the bakery and coffee shop. "This new location appears to be really good for business," she commented, while running her hands along the side of her coffee cup.

Debra beamed. "Business has tripled and I'm so glad."

DebbieCakes was located right on the corner of Main Street, a piece of prime property in Sheraton Beach that had become available a little over a year ago. Competitive bids were sent in from all over the place. Rance was determined to get the spot and had friends in high places that were able to make Debra's dream possible.

The place was large and roomy with plenty of small intimate tables. Customers were sitting on overstuffed chairs near the fireplace talking while others had their eyes glued to their laptop screen. All of them had cupcakes. The pastries were so popular, word had spread. For all of the tourists to the area, a storefront window display of assorted cupcakes was enticing enough to draw even the most health-conscious guru into the store.

"Sedona, Main Street is really growing. They just opened Shoe Divas down on the corner."

"I saw that! I'm definitely going to check it out the next time I'm in town." Right now the only thing on her mind was getting back home to see Keith. He was taking her to Virginia Beach tonight for dinner.

"Bianca told me you're dating a hottie," Debra blurted somewhat abruptly, drawing Sedona from her thoughts.

"Bianca has a big mouth," she mumbled and stuffed her mouth with cake.

She gave her a dismissive wave. "You know as well as I do there are no secrets in this town."

Sedona stared out the window at the man in a red Santa suit standing over a black kettle as she replied, "Yes, but I don't even live here, so why do I need to be part of the local gossip? I could see if I was married to a professional basketball player like you. Don't get me wrong, Keith is far from ordinary, but he's a regular person like me." Her comment was met by a rude snort.

"You're a Beaumont. There is nothing ordinary about that," Debra managed between sips of hot chocolate.

"You know what I mean." The corner of her lips tilted.

"Sooo, are you gonna tell me about your mystery man or not?" she pressed.

It still blew Sedona's mind the way her body leaped to attention at the mere thought of Keith. She caught herself blushing. "Where do I begin? Keith is perfect."

"Perfect?" Debra leaned in close, with one arched eyebrow lifted.

She tilted her head slightly. "Amazing would be a better word," she corrected rather dryly. Sedona then made her sweat another long moment, before she added, "He's funny, confident, smart, deliciously sexy, thoughtful—"

"Dang girl, he's all that?" she interrupted with a curious smile.

"And then some." *Damn that man.* "He is so perfect I'm just waiting for the other shoe to drop."

"Maybe it won't."

"Maybe it will." Sedona sighed and her shoulders slumped a little. "He is everything I have been looking for in a man, but I guess part of me just doesn't believe a man like that really exists twice."

Debra laughed, and picked up her cup, cradling it with two hands as she leaned back against the chair, shaking her head. "You know you sound crazy, right?"

She considered her words, then sighed a little at that. "I probably do. I'm so crazy about him that it scares me. Keith is amazing and the way he makes me feel...," she gave a dramatic shiver. "I just can't believe I met someone like him on a dating site."

"You are a walking testament, or at least you will be if this relationship becomes something permanent."

Her stomach fluttered at the thought.

"Has he told you how he feels about you?" Debra asked, crossing her arms over her breasts and tilting her head.

Sedona shrugged. "I was just thinking about that this morning. I don't know. I mean I know he cares about me and I'm ninety-nine percent sure I am the only woman he's seeing. We're together every single day and I'm either sleeping in his bed or he's in mine and yet we still haven't talked about a future."

"Maybe you should ask."

She snorted before she could stop herself. "I don't want to ruin what we have. I actually like enjoying the moment, but I also want to know if we have a future."

"Then you're gonna have to ask him," Debra insisted.

Sedona met her gaze. "You don't think I'm rushing things?"

"You're asking a woman who met a man on a weekend cruise, and ended up pregnant. Now *that's* rushing," she said biting back a grin.

"No that's what I call skill. I should have you come and teach a seminar on how to snatch an NBA player."

They shared a laugh and then Sedona brought her coffee to her lips and took another sip.

Debra pointed a finger at her. "I think before the two of you get naked again, you need to just ask him what the future holds."

"Then I better do that over the phone because it seems the clothes are off before we hit the top stair."

Her brow quirked. "That good huh?"

"No, it's better," Sedona replied with a saucy grin.

What she had with Keith was so good she never wanted it to end.

♦ ♦ ♦

Keith had been on the main deck of the ship for most of the morning, re-surveying angles, determining the property location for a central intelligence weapon system gun mount.

He carried the tripod to the center line of the ship then locked it in place. He had been right. The last calculations had been considerably off and after losing thousands of dollars, and wasted man hours, the naval engineering department had insisted the calculations be shot all over again. Keith was the only one management trusted to get the job done right.

For the next hour he began shooting laser, determining the coordinates and jotting them in a log book. Usually he had the calculations done in no time, but today — the entire damn day — he couldn't get Sedona off his mind.

He had to tell her the truth. Last night he'd lain awake thinking about them and a future.

He wanted more.

They had fallen into a rhythm that seemed to work for them. Her place or his. Whichever, it didn't matter, just as long as they were together. He loved the sound of her sleeping beside him. He couldn't get enough of the feel of her against him or the sounds she made in response when he played with her breasts.

What they had went beyond sex. They had a connection that stimulated him, his mind, and body. Curling up on the couch together was a turn-on to him and then there were the long deep conversations that seemed to go on for hours that he never grew tired of having. Every day and night only made him want more.

But, there was still that brick wall.

He wanted a future with Sedona and yet until he told her the truth, he couldn't even hint at wanting something more. Not yet. Not now. Not with guilt eating at his chest.

With a long breath, Keith closed the log book. As soon as he went down he would turn the book over for the engineers to review before the ship-fitters could begin assembling the parts for the unit. There were still several other phases involved before the government would come out for final inspection, but this was one of the most critical. Keith loved what he did but there were so many days he missed being out at sea. Although if he had, he never would have had a chance with Sedona.

And he wanted her so bad his chest hurt, but until he told her the truth they'd never have a chance at a future.

"Hey Keith."

"Yo, what's going on Jacob?"

"Just waiting for those last cuts to be approved." He shook his head. "I don't know why they didn't do benchmarks.

Keith nodded. "I agree. It would have made this all so much easy."

Jacob brought a hand up and patted his shoulder. "Son, it's never easy, but I have confidence your calculations are accurate."

"I hope so." He snapped the lock shut on the kit. "How's that wife doing?"

The fifty-something-year-old grinned at the mention of his high school sweetheart. "She's doing great. Chemo has stopped. She's hoping to have enough peach fuzz on her head for Christmas with the kids."

He loved hearing about him and Olivia. They'd been married thirty years and he still had a sparkle in his eyes every time he talked about her. That's what he wanted.

"Make sure you tell her I said hello."

He nodded. "I sure will. She's already talking about baking her apple pies."

Keith licked his lips at the mention. Last year he'd brought in five pies for the holiday Christmas party. They were better than any pie he'd ever tasted before.

Thoughts of spending the holidays with Sedona and her family popped in his head. He sighed, as a feeling of satisfaction washed over him. Christmas was her favorite time of the year and he wanted to make it one of surprise and fulfillment. He planned to do everything he could to keep that smile on her face. "You have a good night."

"You do the same."

He moved toward his vehicle anxious to get home to shower and change. He couldn't wait to touch her again. To taste her soft lips. To feel her soft lush body against his. His cock throbbed at the visual image.

Keith dragged a hand across his jaw. Sedona had his head. Both of them. Yep, he needed to talk to her ASAP so they could take their relationship to the next level.

Chapter 13

Keith took her to a steakhouse in Virginia Beach where the ribeye steaks were to die for. The flavor was so robust she practically ate the entire thing.

By the time they left the restaurant, it was late and yet for a Friday night, Atlantic Avenue was still alive. Shops and bars were open, traffic lights were on and the sidewalks were crowded. Keith suggested they walk along the boardwalk behind the hotels for a bit before they headed to his place. The air was cool, the wind brisk, but not as cold walking along the ocean as one would think. Sedona was wearing a black leather jacket over black slacks and a gold sweater. Boots were on her feet, so they were nice and toasty. His hand at the small of her back ensured that she felt nothing but heat.

"Tired?" Keith asked as he led her down the boardwalk.

Sedona shook her head. "No, I'm wide awake." She walked beside him and listened to the waves washing along the sand. "Thank you for dinner. It was delicious."

"You're welcome, babe."

He was quiet again, something he'd been doing most of the evening, which was strange for Keith since he always seemed to have something to talk about. That was one of the things she really liked about him.

"Is something bothering you?" she asked.

"What makes you say that?"

She shrugged. "Because you've seemed distracted

most of the evening. Like you have something on your mind."

"No, I'm fine really. Just thinking about us." He squeezed her hand. His fingers were large, strong, and very warm.

"What about us?"

"About how much you mean to me." Keith stopped walking and turned to face her.

"I've been thinking the same about you, how important you have become in my life in such a short time." She gave a nervous laugh. "I can't stop thinking about you."

"Neither can I," he growled, then leaned in and covered her mouth with his. The kiss was soft and sensual, filled with so many emotions. She angled her head, giving him better access and brought her arms around his waist. The kiss went on forever as if the world around them stood still, and when she finally drew back they just stood there locked in each other's arms, hearts pounding.

Hand in hand once again, Keith was silent all the way to his car.

"We still going to your place?" she asked as he walked around to her side of the car and opened the door for her.

"No, I like going to yours," he admitted as he waited for her to climb in, then shut the door.

Sedona buckled her seat belt as she waited for him to climb in. A nightclub on the corner was jumping and young people were walking around laughing and talking, half-dressed, and oblivious to the cold.

Keith climbed in and settled behind the wheel.

He turned the key in the ignition and she immediately reached down and pressed the seat

warmers then leaned back comfortably on the seat.
Reaching over, Keith placed a hand to her thigh, and
instead of pulling off, he shifted on the seat.

What Sedona saw raging in his eyes caused her breath
to hitch and her mouth went dry. Something had
changed tonight. What, she wasn't sure, but it was
something major. Keith was behaving differently and the
emotions bubbling up inside of her had intensified. *God,*
she couldn't have looked away if her life had depended
on it.

"Do you like me, Sedona?" he suddenly asked out of
the blue.

"Yes." She bit her lip.

"How much?"

"A lot." She swallowed. "A whole lot." His
expression was solemn. A dark shadow of stubble was
present along his jaw. "I can't wait for my family to meet
you."

"And I'm looking forward to meeting them." He
lifted an eyebrow and leaned closer. "Sweetheart, you're
driving me insane."

He kissed her forehead, then her cheek and finally her
lips before he put the car in gear and peeled away from
the lot.

Sedona took a deep breath. She liked knowing she
was in his head and on his mind. She was anxious to get
Keith home so she could feel his arms around her.

He zipped down the highway, heading back to
Hampton as fast—if not faster—than the law allowed.
Other than the roar of the engine, the only sound in the
car was her shaky breath. He slid his hand into her lap,
his big fingers twined with hers. Words weren't needed.
Instead she was lost in her thoughts, thinking about the
night ahead and what the future would hold for the two

of them. He wanted to talk. The thought had her giddy inside. They were finally going to talk about them. And she couldn't wait.

Minutes later, he was parking in her garage and rushing around to hold the door for her.

"You don't have to open the door for me all the time," she said.

"I have since day one. Why should tonight be any different?"

Because it is. The entire evening had been different in a nail-biting exciting kind of way. She was anxious to hear what was on his mind, but even more desperate to feel him inside of her again. It was a short walk into the house, down the hall and up the stairs. Keith held her hand, leading the way, with her stomach tight in knots.

Would he kiss and make love to her before they talked or after, she wondered? It didn't matter to her either way. One was just as important tonight as the other, so it really didn't matter which was first. She wanted to talk, but at the same time she was dying to feel his hands all over her body.

He led her into her room and once there he swung around and gathered her close. "I'm crazy about you, Sedona."

His confession caused her heart rate to soar. Sedona lifted her gaze and could have sworn she saw something dark, primitive and even a tangle of unfamiliar emotions simmering there. "I feel the same way about you." Her breasts were pressed against him, their hearts thundering together. Something about his energy had shifted. He seemed restless and uneasy. She drew back slightly and asked with a tentative quiver in her voice, "Where do we go from here?"

His lids rose and that's when she saw it. Increased

hunger, pain and something else. Surely it wasn't what she was thinking. What her heart ached for? *Oh God*, a girl could only hope.

"Anywhere you want, just as long as you're in my life," he replied. His eyes, so beautiful and brown, bored into her, scorching its way down the length of her face. Whatever was on his mind was serious and intense. He slid his fingers up and down along her spine, sliding low enough to caress her ass and then she whimpered when he brushed his other hand across her back, holding her in place, while he kissed her long and deep.

Too many hours and days had been spent thinking about him and this moment. Now that it was here, she didn't want to think, didn't want to talk, only feel him against her. Keith had penetrated her mind and heart completely until he was all she thought about. He was gorgeous, funny, thoughtful, compassionate and so many confusing other things at once that she didn't know how to behave anymore. Tonight things had changed, her craving and longing had increased, and right now it was all about what she needed.

"Promise me we'll talk later, but right now I need you to make love to me." She slipped her hands up under the hem of his sweater. His skin was warm and ripped and freaking perfect. When she grazed a thumb over his pecs, Keith drew back, studied her face. Something was happening. Something she couldn't explain. Rightness, anticipation, and a shoebox filled with emotions. But it was mutual and that scared the hell out of her. Sedona was practically holding her breath as she waited.

Finally, Keith swallowed heavily and replied in a low rumble that rippled through her, "Agreed."

He braced her up against the wall and then took her mouth. The kiss was hard, and wild and Sedona gave just as good as she got, tangling her tongue with his, tasting his sweet breath. His lips and tongue were mind-boggling and alluring. Keith tangled his fingers through her hair and angled her back for better access.

She wasn't sure how or when they'd stripped off their clothes. Her eyes snapped to Keith's cock. Her tongue peeked out as she stared. He was perfect, and his erection stood bold, hard and ready. Sedona reached out and swept her long fingers along its length causing Keith to flinch and then he joined in, exploring, stroking her body as well. His rough palms were everywhere—her back, neck and then he found her breasts, encircled them—and when his thumb grazed her nipple, she thought she would have collapsed.

Sedona hadn't known she could feel like this. Wild and reckless. She was flushed with heat and the touch of his hand skimming her inner thighs had her feeling almost feverish. And just when she thought she couldn't take it another moment, he made her feel more.

Keith smoothed his palm along her skin and down to delve between her thighs, cupped her pussy, and made her legs weak. One touch, and she was moaning with pleasure, whimpering with need. He slid a finger through her gentle folds, stroking and caressing before sliding up to stroke her clit. He brought one leg up around his waist and penetrated her deeper. First one finger and then two. He was driving her insane. Keith knew just what she wanted and what it would take to get her there.

Sedona brought her hands up and slid her nails across his back and then dug them into the cheeks of his ass. His cock pressed against her thigh, pulsing with anticipation for what was yet to come.

Oh, she was going to come alright.

"You're wet," he murmured and his nostrils flared.

"It's your fault."

Eyes locked, his fingers continued pumping up inside of her. Filling her. Teasing her. Penetrating her some more. She arched against his hand, while she whimpered and her breathing grew short and heavy. The first climax hit her so hard, it left her shuddering and screaming out his name. "Keith!"

"I love the way you say my name." He made a sound at the back of his throat as he whispered, "That's it baby. Let it go."

Sedona couldn't catch her breath and didn't care. She was shaking, her skin was alive and energized as a result of the sensations rumbling through her. And he didn't give her time to enjoy any of it.

"Again," he murmured and lowered his lips to her breasts, sucking her nipples and sending her pulse pounding. She was already wet, creamy and hot.

"You're so greedy," she whimpered, then arched her back, drawing her nipple further into his mouth. The sensation ripped through her until she felt it at her belly and then between her legs.

"Babe, I love the sounds you make," Keith said and continued kissing and nibbling. Her heart pounded rapidly beneath it. "I want you to come for me again," he coaxed, then raised his head and stared down into her eyes when he rubbed his thumb across her clit. It was swollen and pulsing.

Sedona didn't want to come again. Not yet. She'd rather wait and save her energy for the main course, but it was something about the night, the swirl of emotions, the raw unfamiliar hunger flaming in his eyes that invaded her resistance and wore her down.

"Keith!" His talented fingers had her shuddering with

need as he stroked her.

"That's it babe."

Holding her close, she felt the hard length of him pressing against her, pulsing, waiting patiently. She released a breathless groan, arching into him, wanting, needing.

"All I think about is you," he admitted and buried his face in her hair.

Those words floated through her mind like a gentle caress.

"All I want...need...is you," she confessed.

Keith lifted his head and stared into her eyes.

Sedona wanted him in ways that were a much deeper need than sex. She should have been afraid of what she was feeling and thinking, but instead she embraced it.

Keith took her mouth again and this time his hands were everywhere, sliding along her bare skin, touching her so intimately. He walked her backwards, without breaking the kiss, toward the bed and then gently pushed her down onto the mattress and lay beside her.

Sedona ran her hands up and down his broad back, loving the feel of his muscular body beneath her fingers. She groaned as he lowered his head to her breasts and took first one, then the other nipple into his mouth. His tongue caressed the nipple while he sucked at her sensitive skin and she felt the torch beneath her breasts flaming hotter. Keith slid his tongue all along her body, tasting, exploring every inch as if he couldn't get enough of her, and she felt the same. Over and over he stroked her body, then he was down between her legs sucking and licking until Sedona was panting and shuddering, desperate for release. The first two orgasms were already forgotten and her body was frantic for the next release.

Keith positioned himself between her thighs, then

gazed down at her face. Grabbing her hips, he lifted her off the bed, then thrust inside her heat in one long, powerful stroke.

"Keith!" she moaned and stared into his eyes with no desire to look away. She watched his reaction to their joining. Desire and hunger burned from his gaze. He set the path, hard and deep, with her arms around his neck, and his hands pushing down on her thighs, spreading her wider, allowing him deeper penetration.

And that was when it hit her.

Oh God, help her! She loved him. It wasn't just a physical and mental attraction she felt, Keith had slipped into her heart and wasn't going away. Sedona bit down on her lip to keep from telling him how she felt when what she wanted was to shout her discovery to the world.

Reaching up she ran her finger along his face, down his neck and across his broad shoulders, and then she fastened her lips at his throat, drawing his skin between her teeth before biting him possessively. It was too late for her to walk away. Maybe it had been from the beginning. All Sedona knew was the man she loved was holding her, and nothing else mattered.

Pleasure was coiling tight, release was close. The air was burning her lungs. Keith drove hard, thrusting again and again. Locking her legs around his hips, Sedona took him deeper.

"Look at me," he ordered, in a low, strained growl. "I want to see your face when you come."

Sedona looked up at him as a gasp of pleasure escaped her lips. She couldn't look away. She clung to him, and it went on and on, hard and fast. His hands gripped her hips, guiding her, holding her in place while he continued to pound deeply inside her.

"I love you," slipped from Sedona's tongue. She continued to stare into his eyes and saw the flash of pleasure as his body stiffened and then shuddered with release.

◆ ◆ ◆

He couldn't do it.

He had every intention of telling her the truth, but the evening had been so perfect, he didn't want to ruin it, and then Sedona had confessed she loved him and at that point Keith was determined to end the night on a positive note. But it was now morning and as soon as Sedona was awake, nothing was going to stop him from telling her the truth.

Keith buried his face in her hair, drawing in the scent of her. He loved her. There was no point in denying it. He loved Sedona. And he wanted more. They were in love and the only way they had a chance was if he told her the truth. She had become his addiction. After years of dating countless women, Sedona was the one Keith couldn't get out of his head or heart. She was like a drug and he wanted her nonstop, not just her body, but also her mind, and her soul. Every day and night, forever. It had been a long time coming and now that it was finally here he was never letting her go.

Keith just hoped like hell Sedona would find it in her heart to forgive him. He was afraid of losing what they had when he told her the truth, but if he wanted to move forward—and he did—he couldn't keep the truth from her any longer even though the thought of hurting her bothered him.

Possessively, he pulled her tightly into his arms and eventually dozed off.

Hours later he heard his phone ringing and Sedona stirred in his arms. "Go back to sleep," he whispered and pressed a kiss at her collarbone. Keith slipped out from underneath her, found his pants and retrieved it.

"Hey, Keith, this is Jacob. The engineers approved your calculations. They want us all in today."

He hated working Saturdays, but he knew duty called and there was no way he was letting them make any cuts to the mount without him. "I'll be there." Keith hung up and reached down for his clothes. Sedona rolled over.

"You leaving?" she murmured.

He tipped his head to the side and stared at her half-lidded gaze. Her hair was tussled. She looked like a woman who had been thoroughly made love to. The sight caused his blood to boil hot, his cock once again was at full mast.

"Only for a few hours. I'll be back as soon as I can." He picked his clothes up off the floor and padded over to the bed. "But when I get back, I want us to talk about us, with our clothes on." A handful of emotions flickered in her eyes. Leaning over, Keith brought his lips down over Sedona's, losing himself in the taste of her mouth. "And when we get done talking, I want you to tell me you love me again."

"Okay," she purred, then her eyes strayed down to his erection. Sedona reached out and wrapped her fingers around his cock, and he hissed a breath in pleasure.

"How about one more for the road?" she cooed.

"Anything for you, babe," Keith decided.

Work would just have to wait.

Chapter 14

Sedona was in love.

Hours later she was sitting in her sunroom staring off at the manicured lawn, thinking about Keith.

She loved him being here. In her life. In her bed. He was already in her heart.

She was in love.

Sedona bit her bottom lip as she remembered blurting out her feelings in the heat of the moment. The response was met by silence, but the raw look in Keith's eyes told her he had so much to tell her. And she couldn't wait. Tonight they were going to finally talk about them. The direction of her future was only mere hours away. She drew in a shaky breath and then reached for her cup of peppermint tea.

Every morning she thanked God for bringing him into her life.

Keith had swept her off her feet, allowed her to be vulnerable and exposed, and in return she had fallen hard. So hard her feelings for him surpassed anything she had ever felt for Webb. Not that she hadn't truly loved him. There was never a question about that. Instead with maturity and experience Sedona had learned how to love again.

With a smile, she rose and carried her mug to the kitchen, then padded through the house and up the flight of stairs. They were leaving for Richmond on Christmas Eve and she had yet to find a pair of black designer boots.

Sedona walked down the hallway and stepped into one of the two spare bedrooms. It was a room Sage preferred whenever she drove down for a visit. For a woman who loved being close to the water, it was a wonder she hadn't made the decision to relocate to Virginia Beach or even Sheraton Beach. But the dealership was her life and despite butting heads with Rush, automobiles was one passion she wasn't letting go.

A smile tipped Sedona's lips at the sight of the yellow elephant positioned on the bed. For a feisty little woman, Sage had a soft passionate side that very few knew about. One was her love for stuffed animals.

She padded across the carpeted floor and over to the walk-in closet. Her eyes traveled along the boxes that lined the floor of the closet then up to her summer wardrobe hanging in the closet. One of these days she was going to spend the day organizing her clothes the way her garage had been done. Maybe then Sedona wouldn't have such a hard time finding what she was looking for.

Kneeling down on the floor, she reached for one of the boxes and peeked inside, then put it back and reached for the next. Somewhere in one of them was a pair of expensive black suede boots she was dying to wear to her father's company Christmas party. Her heart fluttered as she thought about finally introducing Keith to the rest of the Force MDs. Rush, Roman, Remy, Reese, Rance, and Sage. Half African-American, half Samoan, and all doctors...each in their own unique way.

While she released a long shaky breath, Sedona reached for a smaller box and when she looked inside her breath stalled.

Inside were tons of letters and cards Webb had given her since they'd first started dating. Sedona removed several envelopes and stared down at his penmanship. They used to joke all the time that he had chicken scratch. While smiling, she thumbed through the letters and stared down at the dates and the APO addresses. When she recognized one from Japan, she stopped, opened the envelope and reached for the card inside. Tears brimmed Sedona's eyes as she gazed down at the poem, "Unconditional Love". Something Webb always said about their relationship. As she opened the card something fell onto the floor. She reached down and picked up a photograph.

As she shifted, curling her legs beneath her, Indian-style, Cocoa appeared at her closet door. She stroked her thick coat of fur while she stared down at a photo. It was Webb on the ship deck making silly faces into the camera along with four other sailors. Sedona giggled and took her time reminiscing back on those days. A tan t-shirt strained around the biceps of his arms. He used to tell her whenever he thought about sex he'd go burn off steam in the weight room. His gorgeous physique was proof of all the hours he'd spent trying to shift his energy and thoughts to something less sexual. His faithfulness to their relationship had never been in question. With a smile, Sedona was skimming the faces of the other four when her eyes flew by one that caused her gaze to zip back and widen with alarm.

Keith?

"No...no way," Sedona whispered and shook her head with disbelief.

Brow bunched, she drew the photograph closer needing to be absolutely sure. A buzz cut, deeply imbedded dimple at his cheeks, full lips and eyes she'd dreamed about every night for the last few weeks, but it was his signature smile—there was no denying it. He was younger and quite a bit thinner, but it was him. Hands shaking, Sedona flipped the photo over and gazed down at the names scribbled on back and the betrayal sliced even deeper at her gut. Webb. Mallory. Johnson. Pope. And as she stared down at the last name, Sedona released a shudder.

Falcon.

Webb's friend Falcon was the same man she had allowed herself to fall in love with.

Horror filled her chest.

Quickly she flipped the photo over and stared at Keith's grinning face again, her heart pounding like a drumbeat in her chest.

This was the same man who she couldn't get off her mind, who had her thinking about a future with babies and a white picket fence. He was also the same man who Webb had – on countless occasions – spoke about being right there, having his back. The same man who had attended his funeral and hand delivered his final letter to her.

For the next few hours Sedona opened and reread countless letters and cards. All the times Webb had mentioned Falcon and their tours together and not once had she put the connection together.

How had she missed the connection?

The sad part was Keith had known all along whom she was. Why hadn't he told her? Not once – in all of the intimate moments they had shared – had he said anything.

Sedona leaned back against the wall and stared up at the handbags on the top shelf as she tried to remember meeting him at the funeral, and tried to ignore the tears sliding down her cheek.

"I'm so sorry for your loss. Webb was a great friend. He'll

definitely be missed."

She had been distraught, sitting there at the grave, watching Webb's body be lowered into the ground when Senior Master Chief Keith Falcon had handed her the letter. As soon as she had glanced down at her name in that familiar penmanship, she lost it. Sage had rushed to her side and Sedona had no memory of what had happened the rest of the day. The sealed envelope had sat on her dresser for nearly a week before she had Sage sit with her while she read the last letter she'd ever received from Webb.

"Sweetheart, if you're reading this letter then that means God decided to call me home…"

She had spent hours reading that letter over and over. Webb reminded her of the first time he realized he loved Sedona was when she had blue raspberry cotton candy on the end of her nose. Webb went on to thank Sedona for supporting his career and loving him unconditionally despite being hundreds of miles apart. And at the end of the letter he asked her to promise him that someday she would love again.

Sedona had spent months reading that letter and all the others in the box over and over until she had them committed to memory, so why had she never made the connection to Falcon?

Betrayal simmered through her veins. Why had he lied to her?

Frustrated, Sedona reached for a pair of sneakers, and rose from the floor. She needed to know the truth.

♦ ♦ ♦

Keith pulled his car into the designated parking space in front of his townhouse and drew a weary breath.

It had been a long day—longer than he had intended—at the shipyard. The cuts had been made, the inspector had rechecked the calculations, and thanks to Keith they had come up almost as accurate as possible. Not that he had taken all the credit. He believed in a team effort. A team was only as strong as their weakest link and it was his job to make sure there weren't any. The cuts had been completed and the mount was ready for the welders to start the next phase.

On the drive home Keith called Sedona and told her he was going home to shower and change, then he would be over. They had a lot to talk about and he was ready.

Tonight Keith not only planned to tell her the truth, but he was also going to tell her he loved her as well. Not telling her last night after she had confessed how she felt had been the hardest thing he had ever done, but he wanted it to be right. Well tonight, there was no more stalling. Tonight was the night.

Keith climbed out of his vehicle and made his way to the door, and startled when he found Sedona sitting on the top step with her hands buried inside the pockets of a long, dark winter coat. "Hey baby, what are you doing here?"

"I have something to say that couldn't wait."

Keith watched the multitude of emotions skate across her face as she rose. None he was familiar with. One in particular scared the hell out of him.

"Why didn't you tell me who you really were?"

Damn. Shock filled his lungs. Although he had known it was just a matter of time before she'd found out the truth, he had hoped he would have gotten to her first.

"Sedona, I didn't know how to tell you."

She shook her head. "So you decided to deceive me instead?"

The hurt in her voice twisted at his gut.

"I was planning to tell you the truth," he managed to get out.

Sedona turned her face up, disappointment was etched in the lines around her eyes. "All this time you knew who I was. I talked about Webb, you saw his photograph, and yet you never said anything."

Keith dragged a hand through his short cropped hair. "I know and I'm sorry, but babe I swear to you I was gonna talk to you tonight."

Confusion and anger filled her eyes. "You just can't stop lying, can you?" Sedona tried to brush past him, but Keith reached out, grabbed her forearm and dragged her to him.

"Can you please give me a chance to explain?" The question hovered in the air.

Wrapping his arms around her, Keith held her as tightly as he could, but Sedona pushed hard against his chest and stepped away from his embrace.

"Please, babe. I can make this right."

Sedona shook her head. "You've had plenty of time to explain!"

"I was wrong. I'll admit that. I should have been honest in the beginning, but answer this...would you have let me get this close if you had known who I was?"

"I guess we'll never know now, will we?" she said quietly.

"Sedona, I know you're angry and you have every right to be but, babe, we've got something good here." Keith moved toward her again, but she backed away.

"We *had* something good." Sedona gave him a sad, yet lethal glare. "Stay away from me, Keith. I have nothing else to say to you."

Keith swore long and hard as he watched her walk

toward her car. Residents were moving around the complex, and therefore, now was not the time to plead his case. Sedona was too angry. Besides, she was right. He had screwed up. He should have been honest with her from the beginning.

Keith watched her pull out the parking lot before he went inside. Dread settled into his chest. Now what?

Shrugging out of his jacket, he tossed it onto a large recliner in the living room, then headed down the small carpeted hallway into an outdated galley kitchen. He needed a beer while he tried to think of a plan before he approached Sedona again. It was clear forgiveness was going to take more than a sincere apology.

Keith reached into the refrigerator and swore under his breath as he removed a can, then he moved to a small bistro style table and took a seat. As he sipped his beer all he could think about was the disappointment he saw in Sedona's eyes. All because of him. He never meant to hurt her. Now he needed to find a way to get her to trust him again.

By the time he crumpled the third can and tossed it into the trash, Keith decided to give Sedona a chance to cool off, then he was coming back to stake his claim. What they had only came once in a lifetime. She made him feel whole, and he wasn't about to let that go.

Chapter 15

"Are you okay? I've been trying all day to reach you!"
Sedona heard the concern in Energi's voice and immediately felt guilty. A few years ago, her younger brother had committed suicide after struggling for years with depression. When Energi had been unable able to reach her, it was probably the first thing that had come to mind. Sedona loved herself too much to do anything that final, however, taking a tennis racket upside Keith's head didn't sound like a bad idea.

"I'm really sorry. I woke up this morning feeling like I needed a day to myself."

"Nothing's wrong with that but next time at least shoot me an email or something," Energi snapped and must have regretted her response because she quickly blurted, "I'm sorry. I shouldn't have said that."

"No apology needed. I should have at least called you. It's common courtesy." Especially since she'd heard Energi ringing the doorbell shortly after ten, which she had ignored.

Sedona tossed another log into the fireplace, then curled back onto the large cream-colored couch. Typically she wasn't rude, but she just hadn't been herself lately. "Are you still in the office?"

"No, I locked up on my way to class, but while I have you on the phone, let's go over a few things."

"Sure. I'm all ears," she replied.

The two went over her schedule and finalized the

Women's Leadership and Empowerment Conference at Georgia Southern University, being held MLK weekend. Pauline Battle, the founder of the Women's Empowerment Network, had reached out to her, and Sedona truly felt honored. She and Energi discussed marketing, and then went over the details of another speaking engagement scheduled before New Year's Eve.

At the close of the call, Sedona clicked End and placed her phone onto the end table, beside a half-full cup of coffee. She had almost forgotten she'd brewed it. She took a sip of the lukewarm hazelnut blend and glanced around the room. The Christmas lights Keith had strung were twinkling around the windows. The large tree in the corner was blinking merrily at her. What was supposed to have been the best Christmas she'd had in years was turning out to become one of her worst.

She hadn't heard a peep out of Keith in two days. Even if he had tried to reach her, she would have ignored his calls. How could she have been so blind to have allowed herself to get so caught up in that mess? Was she really that desperate to fall in love again that she had turned a blind eye, ignoring all the signs?

Sedona took another sip and pondered that thought. The moment Keith told her he'd served in the Navy, she should have started asking questions, because in the midst of the discussion she would have known. Instead, she blindly rushed into his arms and believed they had a future together.

"How could I have been so stupid?" she whispered.

With a scowl and another sip, she forced herself to push aside the blame. There was no way she was going to put it all on herself. Keith had always been in control. He knew who she was. He had known all along.

Sedona released a string of obscenities under her

breath that would have caused her mother to frown. All the hours she had spent getting to know him and she really didn't know him at all even though her heart said otherwise. Keith was compassionate, funny, sexy, thoughtful.... She let that thought trail off because if he was all those things, why had he lied?

You should have let him explain.

Briefly she closed her eyes, fighting back tears. After she had discovered his deception, she couldn't bear to hear anything else he had to say and yet now she was still trying to figure it out. *Why? Why?*

No matter what scenario she came up with it, it didn't at all explain the man she had spent the last few weeks, in his arms, in her bed. Her mind raced with thoughts of all the things she had allowed Keith to do to her body. Even now she could still feel him buried inside her, pumping his hips with deep confident strokes. The memories alone were enough to drive her insane.

"I still can't believe he played me like that," she said out loud, then released a long groan. She had been doing that a lot. Talking to herself. Cocoa looked over at her from her pet bed, then went back to licking herself. Tonight wasn't the first time. Sometimes talking to herself just seemed to make things better.

"He knew all along, and not once did he say anything to me," she spat as she stared down at the log burning in the fireplace. What bothered her most was that despite what Keith had done, she missed him like crazy.

"Really Donie?"

He didn't deserve a second of her thoughts and yet he was all she could think about. In such a short time, Sedona had allowed him to get under her skin and even worse, he'd gotten past the wall she'd kept around her heart. As a result, what she'd hoped never happened again, had happened. Her heart had been broken.

"Damn you!" she screamed and Cocoa hurried out of the room. "Sorry Cocoa!" she called after her.

So much for the pity party.

Sedona rose from the couch and carried the cup to the kitchen. This wasn't her first rodeo. She was a big girl and had been hurt before. The heartbreak she felt, would eventually fade. As she lowered the cup in the sink, Sedona tried to convince herself Keith wasn't worth another thought. Unfortunately, her heart refused to listen.

◆ ◆ ◆

Keith gave Sedona two days. Enough time to calm down, at least he hoped. By the second evening, he got off work, came home and changed into a clean pair of blue jeans, a heavy thermal, and headed out the front door. On the way to his car, he called Sedona and was surprised she'd finally answered. He wasted no time.

"You might as well get ready Sedona. I'm on my way over."

"What? Keith, don't—"

Gently he cut her off. "We'll talk when I get there." As he ended the call, he felt a glimmer of hope.

On the drive over, he did the same thing he'd been doing since Saturday—trying to think what he would say because it was going to take a great deal just to get her to listen and not slam the door in his face. Sedona was independent and stubborn, two qualities he loved about her and also the reason why he refused to accept it was over between them.

Keith parked, strode up to her front door and rang the bell.

He was already prepared for the cold glare and a smart remark coming from her lips. She had every right, he decided. After ringing the bell a second time, he reached inside his pocket for his phone and called her number.

"What?" she barked.

"Open the door, Sedona."

"Why?" she replied stiffly.

"So we can talk." Keith spoke calmly.

There was a long pause before Sedona muttered, "I'm around back." And the phone went dead.

Keith stuck his phone back into his pocket, drew a breath, then strolled across the lawn toward the rear of the property. Lights flooded from the deck and along the stairs leading to the French doors. The fire pit had been lit. The waterfall was on and the tranquil sound was enough to make him want to walk over to the cabana, kick back and relax. Sedona was already sitting up on the elevated sofa, her back propped up against a pile of pillows.

"You look cozy," he said as he walked cautiously while studying her.

Sedona was wearing a white sweat suit, thick green bootie socks on her feet. Her hair was brushed away from her face, showcasing her large sable eyes, finely arched eyebrows and clear brown skin, and she looked sexy as ever.

"You wanted to talk, so talk," she urged with a sweep of her hand.

She was on the defense and probably had her guard up, not that he blamed her after what he had done. Keith decided not to take a seat on the couch, and instead he leaned against the thick posts and looked at her. Sedona immediately rolled her eyes and trained her vision toward the fire pit instead.

"You're wasting your time. Personally, there really isn't anything left to talk about."

His heart plummeted at the sharp tone of her voice. "I think we have a lot to talk about."

"Really?" she sniffed. "And what are you planning to lie about this time?"

Sedona was so cute when she was mad.

Leaning forward, he reached down, grabbed her ankles, and despite Sedona's cry of protest, Keith slid her across the cushion, to the end of the chaise lounge until she was sitting on the edge and his legs were straddling hers.

He locked his eyes on her stubborn face. "Sedona, I didn't lie, but you're right, I didn't tell you the truth either."

"And that's supposed to make it all better?" Her voice held a hard edge. Nothing about her gaze had softened. Her eyes were still cold enough to send a chill racing down his spine.

Keith was thankful for the fire pit.

"So let's analyze this…" she began. "You knew who I was, but yet you made the decision to hide your connection to Webb from me."

Damn, she sounds like a psychologist.

"Are you gonna let me talk?"

She pursed her lips, clearly unhappy with his persistence. "Go ahead and talk, but you're wasting your time."

His confidence slipped a few notches, but he wasn't going to let it stop him. She was angry. He got that. Hopefully, she was open to hearing his explanation.

"When I first saw your photo, I admired you from a distance even though I was attracted. But when you reached out to me, I knew I had to meet you, even if to just say hi and to tell you who I was."

"Then why didn't you?" Sedona thrust her chin in a gesture of defiance.

"Because once I saw your smile, and your beautiful face, I just couldn't tell you." Keith took a deep breath. "Not yet. Not before I had a chance to get to know you without you first knowing who I was."

"And you don't think that was selfish?"

"Yes, it was selfish, but I didn't want my connection to Webb to complicate me getting to know you."

Sedona crossed her arms and glared up at him. "So you decided to enter my life under false pretenses." It wasn't a question.

He lowered his voice and brushed his knuckles across her cheek. "How do you feel about me?"

She pushed his hand away. "That's not important."

"It *is* important. Sedona, you reached out to me, which meant you were ready to move on with your life."

"My cousin reached out to you," she countered.

"I doesn't matter how it began. It began, and it's been an amazing ride."

"But it's been one big lie," she whispered.

Sedona dropped her eyes. Keith placed a hand at her chin and tilted her face so she had no choice but to look at him. "Everything that has happened between us is real." He studied her face, searching for a glimmer of hope, but there was nothing. "Are you telling me if you had known who I was you never would have gone out with me?"

The tip of her tongue darted out and slicked over her bottom lip. "Yes, no, maybe, but under different circumstances."

"Different in what way?"

Sedona shifted slightly on the couch. "If I had known who you were, I would have asked you about your friendship with Webb and his last days."

"Then what stopped you?" He probed and took a seat on the couch beside her. "After I delivered that letter, at any time you could have reached out to the unit and asked me those same questions, but you didn't. Why is that?"

Sedona dragged a hand across her hair, then released a long shaky breath. "I was a mess back then, spending every hour of the day reading his letters, watching our home videos, staring at his photo. Calling you would have only made his death feel real and I wasn't ready to accept that. In my mind, Webb was still out at sea, and he'd be back eventually."

Keith reached over and placed a hand on Sedona's knee and was pleased she didn't push him away. "You were all Webb ever talked about. He talked about you so much I felt like I knew you." He barked out a laugh. "Sedona, your pictures were everywhere. He'd even read us bits and pieces of your letters. When he asked me to be a groomsman at your wedding, I was excited and jealous at the same time. But, what I was looking forward to most was finally meeting the beautiful Sedona Beaumont. That dude loved you so much at times I was jealous. I wanted what he had."

Sedona tilted her head and met his eyes, a sad smile curling the corners of her mouth.

Keith searched her eyes before he took her hand in his. "I messed up. I get that, but I don't want to lose us," he told her softly.

"I need time."

"To do what? Talk yourself out of being with me," he snapped, starting to get irritated.

"No, time to get over feeling deceived!" she snapped, then paused and drew a long breath before continuing, "Everything's been happening so fast. I need time to really understand what it is I'm feeling."

Still holding her hand, Keith rose and looked down at Sedona as he asked, "How do you feel about me?"

That stubborn look was plastered firmly back in place. "That's not fair."

"Rarely is anything ever fair in love and war."

She shook her head. "Tough, I won't be pressured."

He cupped her chin again. "Look at me because I want no mistake about what I'm getting ready to say to you."

Her breath hitched.

"I'm crazy about you, Sedona, and those feelings began long before I saw your photo on the dating site."

"Is that why you lied to me?" she challenged.

Here we go again.

"Babe, look. I know you're still pissed with me. I should have been honest. I'm sorry that I wasn't, but at this point does it really matter? I'm crazy about you and as much as you try to act like you don't, I know you love me."

She looked as if she wanted to say something. Her lips quivered, then hardened before she finally shook her head, sending her wild curls bouncing. "I think that maybe I was caught up in the moment."

He chuckled. "I've seen your face when I make love to you. I know the way your breath hitches every time I stroke your breasts, the mewing sounds you make when my tongue slides across your clit. I know you love me, so why give up what we have because of one small hiccup in our relationship?"

She stared at him, eyes blinking but the rest of her

frozen. He wasn't sure which direction the conversation was headed.

"The fact that you can stand there and discount what you've done as a hiccup means we really don't have anything else to talk about."

She pushed him out of her way, then rose and headed over to the fire pit and started putting the fire out. Keith stood there, hands in his pocket, admiring how even in a shapeless sweat suit, Sedona still managed to cause his body to stir.

"You probably should leave."

"Why?"

She whipped around. "Because I'm going inside."

In three long strides, Keith caught her arm and turned her slightly so Sedona could see his face and especially the determination in his eyes as he spoke.

"Babe, do you really think all this has been easy for me?"

"What are you talking about?"

"You. Webb. His death. None of what has been happening between us has been easy. I tried to resist you because I knew what you'd meant to my boy, and yet I couldn't. I spent many nights tossing and turning and feeling so guilty."

Her brow bunched with confusion. "Why do you feel guilty?'

"Because Webb was my boy. Ride or die. We were thick as thieves. All he did was talk about you. And that night was no exception. He had been clowning me about wearing a tuxedo and how you had insisted that all of the groomsmen wear pink shirts."

He noticed the way her lip quivered.

"And that's when we got word about the explosion in the engine room. Webb and his crew sprang into action.

He was responsible for damage control..., that's what the Navy had trained him to do," Keith growled and he felt his nostrils flare. "By the time I managed to get down there, the engine room was filled with smoke and flames. Three of us went in, intent only on rescue, and I was the one who found Webb lying there unconscious. When I tried to drag him out, a bulk-head fell from the ceiling and crushed my ankle."

Sedona's eyes were wide with horror. "What... that's how you got that limp?"

Keith nodded and released his hold. Sedona stepped out of his reach, hugging herself while he shoved his hands inside his pockets. "I refused medical attention until I knew Webb was gonna be okay. No one would tell me he was dead. One of the hull techs said Webb was standing near the engine, trying to put out the fire when a second explosion sent the engine door flying off its hinges." For months, nightmare images of Webb's crumbled body played in his head. The stench of charred flesh still burned his nostrils. According to the investigative report, the impact to the skull had killed Webb instantly.

Tears stung Keith's eyes, not that he gave a damn.

"I didn't know," Sedona said, lips trembling, then she turned her back to him and everything was silent. The only sound was labored breathing.

It was Sedona who finally broke the silence. "I think it's time I went inside."

"Before you go, can you answer one thing for me?" Keith asked and hoped he was taking the right approach. "Everything we've experienced... every emotion... did that feel real?"

She twirled around, blinking as she asked, "What does that—"

"Please, just answer the question," he said, then drew an unsteady breath and waited.

Sedona shuddered and finally whispered, "Yes."

"That's what I thought." Keith hugged her close, then swooped in, expecting her to push away, instead Sedona met him halfway, her mouth molding to his, her tongue dancing along his. Cupping the back of her head, he crushed her to him then swept deeper into her sweet mouth and kissed her thoroughly. Their lips clung to each other and went on and on before he finally found the strength to let her go.

Pulling back abruptly, he whispered, "Think what you want, Sedona, but what we have is far from over."

Sedona's eyes widened and her lips trembled, but no words came out before she turned on the balls of her feet and fled inside the house.

Keith waited until he heard the lock turn before he retreated and headed back across the lawn to his car. He felt a twisting sensation at the pit of his belly. Yep. Things were far from over.

Was it so wrong to have wanted to be with a woman who made him forget about everything except the way she made him feel? Was it wrong for wanting a fair shot with a woman he had admired from a distance for years? Yes, he had been wrong for not telling her who he was because he wanted a chance for her to first see him for who he was, not his connection to Webb.

It had taken Keith years to find love, and he refused to give up that easily. Maybe now was not the time, but tomorrow, he was making his intentions known.

And he knew just the place.

Chapter 16

Sedona was sitting on the couch watching the mingling crowd. The Beaumont Automotive Group's Christmas party was in high gear.

Family, friends, employees were all around laughing, talking, drinking and she wished she was back at home curled up on her window seat, staring out at the wind whipping leaves along the lawn, while she hoped for a white Christmas.

Instead she was at her parent's house pretending to feel festive when in reality her heart ached. As much as she wished she didn't, she missed Keith.

Her eyes traveled across the large great room where Rance and Debra were standing arm in arm and she scowled. The couple met on a four-day cruise and fell in love. Why couldn't love be that easy for her? Why'd things have to be so damn complicated?

Sedona pushed the thought aside and forced herself to plaster on a smile and go mingle even though she was feeling in total harmony with Scrooge.

While she sipped eggnog, she nodded and laughed with guests, and faked holiday cheer. And after an hour of being phony, Sedona found a seat on a sofa in the living room and groaned inwardly. It was going to be one long afternoon.

"Merry Christmas!"

She jerked, startled, and looked up into her sister's

eyes. "Sage, you scared me," she managed over the blaring Christmas music.

"Sorry, I called your name twice but you didn't answer," she replied sheepishly. "Here, this is for you."

Sedona noticed the beautifully wrapped box in her proffered hand. Smiling, she put the glass of egg nog on the coffee table and took it from her. "I put your gift under the tree," she informed her then pointed out into the foyer where a huge twelve foot tree stood.

Sage sank down onto the linen sofa beside her. "I'll get it later. Now open it."

Despite how depressed she was feeling, Sedona smiled and gently ripped at the gold foil paper. She never could understand why something so beautiful was made to be destroyed in a matter of seconds. Carefully she opened the box, then reached inside as she glared at her younger sister. "Really?"

She held up a leather riding strap.

Sage chuckled loudly. "*What*? I was just trying to add some spice to your life! How was I to know you were gonna dump the dude before Christmas? I mean really, Donie, you could have at least waited until after you collected your Christmas presents from him."

She frowned playfully. "That's something you do. Not me."

"Might as well get your money's worth," she mumbled under her breath as their great-uncle Chris walked by. "Hey Uncle Chris!" Sage cried and nudged her sister on the arm.

Sedona turned her eyes on her and said, "And I didn't dump him, I just decided we needed a break."

"Because he lied?"

Sedona nodded. "Yes, because he lied, and you've got a lot of nerve. Where's your man?"

Sage waved a heavily jeweled wrist. "I'm too freaky and nasty. No man is gonna put up with me."

Sedona laughed. "That's because you're too busy always trying to be the man in the relationship."

Sage shrugged beneath a blue cowl-neck sweater. "Somebody's gotta do it."

Sedona rolled her eyes. Her sister had a lot to learn about relationship, not that she was one to talk. "You are hopeless."

"Hey, I can't help it if it's gonna take a special man to catch my attention," she said tightly.

"Special? You mean special Ed," she teased.

Sage chuckled in good spirit. "He's probably gonna have to knock me over the head."

"You're probably right," Sedona agreed and laughed.

Sage was what she called a sexy tomboy. Boots, jeans, leather, but you had to force her to wear a dress. Sedona laughed inwardly as she remembered the last time her mother had insisted, and Sage sulking the entire evening. One of their father's employees walked over and she and Sage jumped into a conversation about a car she hoped to sell.

Sedona went back to exploring the box. Her treacherous mind was all too willing to offer up possible ways she and Keith could have used the explicit goodies inside.

Don't even go there.

She had spent practically an entire night crying her eyes out and every emotion she had felt had been about Keith. She was crazy in love with him and yet nothing good could ever come out of their relationship. She needed trust and that was something he couldn't offer her.

"You still haven't told me what it was Keith lied

about," Sage asked as if she had read her mind.

"Maybe later." She definitely wasn't going to tell her now. Not with all the people surrounding them, even though no one was listening. "Nothing worth ruining the holiday over." She looked inside the box again and shook her head. "And to think I spent all that money buying you that leather bolero jacket you were wanting."

"You did?" Sage's eyes widened, then she scurried off in those ridiculously high-heeled stiletto boots to search under the tree. It wouldn't take long to find. The whole family knew Sedona always wrapped her gift with silk ribbons she'd twirled with her kitchen shears.

Sedona put the lid onto the box and slipped it up under the end table away from virgin eyes, then went back to sipping her eggnog. Her father had hired a Santa Claus and he was in the other room with the daughter of one of Rush's managers, sitting on his lap. As she watched them, Sedona couldn't resist a grin because when she had first arrived the seven-year-old had latched onto her for the first hour and had practically talked her head off. Eventually someone was going to have to rescue poor Santa.

Sedona adored children and wanted some of her own, but at the rate her love life was going that might never happen. Unfortunately, that didn't stop her traitorous mind from imagining a child with Keith's butter-brown skin and her dark eyes.

Abruptly, Sedona rose and carried her empty cup into the kitchen where a staff was working dutifully to ensure everything was perfect for the evening.

The smell of her mother's pecan pie sent Sedona into the dining room seeking at least a sniff. She stepped into the room and spotted her baby brother. By the time he had ended the R-rated phone conversation, Sedona shook and mumbled, "One woman is never going to be enough for you, is it?"

Remy laughed. "Something like that."

She reached for the knife and gave him a hard stare. "You're hopeless."

With a hearty chuckle, Remy moved toward her in black slacks and a charcoal gray turtleneck that emphasized all the hours he spent in the gym.

He ran a hand over his wavy hair that was hanging loosely around his shoulders. "Donie, there are just too many beautiful women out there."

With five brothers and a sister who was always competing to be the man, Sedona often felt in a minority all of her own.

"You have fun with that," she commented with a humorless smile. Remy scowled and gave her a dismissive wave then moved to join the others.

Sedona cut a slice of pie and placed it on a small plate, then reached down for a fork. The strain of Michael Jackson's, "I Caught Mama Kissing Santa Claus" filled the air as she stepped into the large kitchen. She went over to talk to her mother's sister, Deidre, and they were looking at baby pictures when Rance towered into the room. Sedona saw the pained expression on his face. "What is it?"

"There's someone here to see you."

"Who is it?" she asked, but Rance had already turned and headed back toward the front of the house. Sedona excused herself and as she smoothed down the front of a red wrap dress, she went to find out for herself. As soon as she reached the foyer, Sedona spotted three of her brothers blocking the main entrance.

"What's going on?" she asked. The guests standing close by shrugged, others were just as curious. With a scowl, Sedona pushed between Rance and Remy. It wasn't what she saw, but who that made her pause.

Keith.

She couldn't help the way her breath caught in her throat at the sight of him. "What are you doing here?"

There was that smile she missed so much as he answered, "I came to give you your Christmas present." His husky voice sent tremors along her body.

He stepped forward holding, a small decorated box.

Sedona stepped out onto the large porch and shivered when she remembered she wasn't wearing her wool coat. She folded her arms across her chest and said softly, "Really, you traveled this far to do that?"

"Actually I'm on my way to Charlottesville to spend the holiday with my mama."

He looked so cute standing there in dark pleated slacks and a pink and brown sweater beneath a leather jacket. Sedona had to resist the urge to jump into his arms. "How did you know where to find me?" Her eyes narrowed suspiciously on his handsome face.

"It wasn't hard to figure out," he said with a wink that caused her brow to bunch with wonder. "Remember, we were planning to make this trip together." He brought his hand up and down along her arm, warming it beneath the soft silky material.

For a long moment they stood there just staring at each other, saying nothing. Sedona forgot they weren't alone until she heard someone clearing their throat. She turned to find three pairs of eyes glaring at them.

"Donie, who is that?"

She glanced over at Keith and said, "This is a friend of mine."

"That's not what he asked you. Who is he?" Rance stepped out onto the porch. Sedona groaned. He was trying an intimidation tactic by towering over them.

With a long breath she held up a hand. "None of your business. Keith, come inside with me." She should have just sent him on his way, but being that Keith had come bearing gifts the least she could do was hear him out. However, instead of following her to the door, Keith stepped over to Rance and extended his hand.

"Whassup man? I'm Keith Falcon." He stood there calm and collective, waiting for Rance. Sedona grinned. Keith didn't appear to be the least bit intimidated.

Rance eventually nodded and shook his hand. With a hand at her hip, Sedona mouthed behind Keith's back, "Behave."

The others grumbled from the double doors.

"Why don't we go inside where it's warm and finish the introductions?" she suggested. This time, Sedona took Keith by the hand. The contact was warm, his strong grip made her yearn for him to touch her all over. She cleared her throat in an effort to keep her head on straight.

Sedona had to practically punch Reed in the arm to get him to move so the two of them could pass. The entire time her heart was beating a mile a second. Not in her wildest dreams had she expected Keith to show up at her parent's house uninvited. Well not really, since he had been invited but then she sort of took his invitation back. Either way she was both pissed he was here and yet happy to see him.

Standing in the foyer, she made the rest of the introductions. Her efforts were met by grunts and mumbling under their breath. No one was blatantly rude, but they weren't warm and fuzzy either.

Sedona spotted Debra sauntering down the wide foyer in a shapely green sweater dress, and breathed a sigh of relief. Assistance was on its way.

"Who do we have here?" Debra asked eyes twinkling with curiosity as she stood beside her husband.

Sedona smiled. "Debra, this is my… friend Keith."

"Friend, huh?" Her brow quirked. "Well, any friend of Donie's a friend of mine." Debra shook his hand and stared up at him smiling.

"We didn't know she was inviting a *friend*," Rance mumbled.

"Since when does she need to ask for permission?" Sage replied with a rude snort as she stepped between Rance and Reed. "Keith, it's nice to finally meet you. I'm Sedona's beautiful younger sister, Sage." She batted her lashes flirtatiously and Sedona felt a tinge of jealousy even though she knew her baby sister meant no harm.

"It's a pleasure to meet you as well," he said and shook her hand.

Sage looked from him, then to Sedona. "Where's our manners? Please give me your jacket and stay awhile."

He raised his hands. "No, really, I'm just stopping through on my way to Charlottesville."

Remy muttered something but when Sedona looked his way, he avoided eye contact.

She sighed. She was supposed to be pissed at Keith, but it wasn't easy, not with him standing there looking so sexy. Every time she looked at him, Sedona felt a tug at her midsection. What was it about this man that made him such a temptation?

She pondered that question while Keith talked to Sage and Debra. Reese walked over, introduced himself and then struck up a conversation.

"Who is this dude?"

Sedona turned to Remy standing beside her.

Ignoring him, Sedona leaned over and placed her gift

under the tree before responding. "I don't ask you about your women."

Remy scoffed. "Because none of them are worth talking about. But the way that dude was looking at you, there's something going on, so what's up with that?"

"What's up is you need to mind your business."

"Donie—"

She held up a hand silencing him. "I'm not listening to this." She stepped over to the others. "Excuse me, but I need to talk to Keith in private." Sedona took him by the arm, and led him down the hall to her father's study at the rear. Once they were inside the room, she closed the door behind them and swung around to glare at him.

"Why are you really here?" she demanded to know.

"I already told you, to bring your Christmas present," he said and grinned.

She wasn't going to let his good looks and charm intimidate her. "When we spoke last night I made it clear I needed time."

There was that irresistible smile again. "Take all the time you need, but in the meantime. I'm gonna make sure you know I'm not going anywhere."

His words caused her insides to stir. Keith was making it so hard for her to stay angry she almost had to remind herself.

"I'm not going to change my mind," she said breathless.

"Yes you will, once you realize I really am a great guy." He reached for her hand. "Sedona, I was wrong. I should have told you who I was from the beginning. I can't change that now, but everything I feel about you... about us, is real."

Not only was his voice husky and arousing, but Sedona caught him staring down at her mouth. Her words caught and faded, "You're complicating things." She licked her lips nervously.

"That's not at all what I'm trying to do." His words stroked up her spine. "All I want to do is love you. That's if you'll let me."

Keith leaned over Sedona and took her mouth, making a mere kiss so much more — deeper and hotter.

Sedona tried to think of every reason why allowing Keith to kiss her was wrong, but for the life of her all she could do was melt in his arms and give in to the taste of his mouth. Damn, she had missed him, craved his kisses and the feel of his arms around her even though she'd just seen him yesterday. As a result, she had no control over the moan escaping her throat.

"I couldn't imagine going another day without holding you in my arms," he whispered.

Keith backed her toward the desk until her hip was resting on the edge. Every swipe of his tongue had her body at attention. Her nipples beaded shamelessly against the fabric of her bra. When he stood between her legs every cell in her body ached for the pleasure only Keith could give her, and then with a single touch of his hand, cupping her breasts, every reason why she needed to stay away from Keith shattered into a thousand pieces.

Keith lifted Sedona onto the desk and she released a helpless whimper. Her dress was bunched at her hips. Keith raised one of her legs up around his waist, then leaned in pressing his erection against her.

"Keith," she choked, voice thick with the conflict of wanting and not wanting him. His hands roamed over her, provoking every nerve ending in her body, while his lips kissed the racing pulse at her throat. "I can't think straight when you do that."

"You don't need to think, only feel."

That was the problem. Keith made her forget why she was angry with him. His skillful hands shattered her guard and made it impossible to think straight. The way he trailed his lips across her neck, had Sedona quivering for something she had no business thinking about, and yet she wanted it anyway.

"I want you in my life, Sedona." The statement spurred a dizzy rush, one that had her arching toward his hand. Keith somehow managed to untie the knot at the side of her wrap dress, then his fingers slipped inside and drifted along her skin before he began stroking her breasts.

His forefinger and thumb found the tip and her mind exploded. He tweaked and caressed her nipples with skill, causing heat to rush to her lower extremities.

When Keith ended the kiss, and stared into her eyes, Sedona was mesmerized by the stark hunger burning in his gaze.

"You want me?"

"No," she said even though her body disagreed.

"Liar," he hissed, then began stroking her inner thigh.

"You're one to talk," she retorted, hoping it would throw him off.

With their eyes locked, he slid his hand higher until he touched her so intimately Sedona had to close her eyes.

He brought his mouth down over hers again, muffling the cry of pleasure that escaped as he caressed and teased her folds through her panties that were growing wetter by the second.

"Talk to me baby. Tell me what you're thinking," he whispered.

She was thinking she wanted so much more.

His fingers slid underneath the crotch of her satin

panties and the muscles at her core pulsed. She was practically holding her breath, waiting, when she heard someone turning the door knob.

Instantly, Sedona jerked off the desk.

"Relax, it's locked," Keith reminded her.

Sedona wiggled, freeing herself of his hold. "I think we need to get back to the Christmas party."

Someone was still trying to get inside. Sedona quickly tied her dress and hurried over to see who it was. She swung the door open and groaned inwardly when she found herself staring at her mother.

Bettye's eyes shifted to the gorgeous man standing behind her daughter. "Who do we have here?" she asked.

"Mom, this is Keith," she said and hoped he didn't notice the tremor in her voice.

Bettye Beaumont was holding a glass of egg-nog. Keith moved to her and brought her free hand to his lips.

"Ma'am it's a pleasure to finally meet you. I see where Sedona gets her good looks."

Sedona rolled her eyes as she watched Keith throw on the charm and win over her mother in a matter of seconds.

Was there any resisting this man?

The way her body had been whimpering for a sexual encore, she was starting to think that resistance was one feat proving to be impossible.

♦ ♦ ♦

He needed to see her.

That's what showing up to the Christmas party unannounced had been about. Keith needed to see Sedona as bad as he needed to take his next breath. They belonged together. He knew it. Now he had to make sure she knew it as well.

The Beaumont bunch was truly a festive bunch. The instant he'd received the lukewarm welcome at the door, he had sensed how protective they were of each other. He liked that.

While Mrs. Beaumont had a talk with Sedona in private, Keith disappeared to the powder room. *Powder room*? The space was larger than the master bathroom at his townhouse, he thought with a chuckle.

After washing his hands, Keith stepped out in the hall and wasn't at all surprised to find one of her brothers standing there, leaning against the wall.

"Which brother are you?" Keith asked.

His stance suddenly became stiff and confrontational.

"I'm Remy. But I'm still trying to figure out who you are."

He wasn't sure how much Sedona had or had not told her family. "What did Sedona say?"

"Donie said it was none of my business," Remy replied with a smile tugging at the scowl on his face.

"Well then I'm gonna have to plead the fifth," Keith said, hands up in surrender. "But I will say this… my intentions are honorable and long term."

Remy gave him a thoughtful look. "My sister has been through hell. That's what all that was about at the door."

Keith nodded. "I understand. All I want to do is love her if she'll have me."

"You know if you do anything to hurt her, you're gonna have hell to pay from all of us."

"Never doubted it for a minute," Keith said with a grin. Remy broke into a smile, then held up a fist and Keith bumped his against him.

A few moments later, Keith was headed toward voices at the rear of the house when he spotted Sedona coming down a double staircase.

She frowned. "There you are! I was looking for you."

"Why, you miss me already?" he grinned.

Sedona snorted as she reached the bottom step. "Not hardly. I just wanted to make sure you weren't robbing us blind while my back was turned." She made a show of patting his pockets.

"Damn, you got me," Keith chuckled.

"Ha-ha, very funny. Don't you have somewhere to be?"

"Yes, now that I've gotten my kiss, and you've gotten your gift, I'm heading out."

Their eyes locked before Sedona dropped her gaze and said, "Let me grab my coat and I'll walk you out to your car."

Keith followed Sedona to the coat closet and helped her slide into a black, wool pea coat. Sage waved and he did the same. She was cute, a younger version of Sedona minus all of the soft delicate curves that filled his dreams.

They walked side by side down the long circular driveway, arms brushing. "I think you impressed my sister."

"That's nice to know, but the only person I care about impressing is you."

He loved the way Sedona dropped her head whenever he complimented her.

Once they reached BMW, Sedona stopped and turned around. Keith pulled her into his arms and captured her mouth, sucking and licking, heat flaring at his loins. Sedona drew back, breathing heavily.

"You have a safe trip to your Mom's." She pushed against him.

"I will and you enjoy the rest of your Christmas." Keith took her hands, pinning them behind her back. As she whimpered in protest, Keith lowered his mouth and locked his lips over hers again, hot, hungry, and consuming. Sedona resisted for only a moment before melting against him. The need to breathe was the only reason why Keith finally pulled away.

"I want to see you when I get back home," Keith said as his body ached with need.

Sedona's eyes widened and he could feel her struggling for control. "I don't know." His eyes locked on hers and one word scrolled through his thoughts — mine.

"Quit fighting it, Sedona," he blurted. "We need to talk. If your brothers weren't ready to hogtie me I'd put you in my car and never let you out of my sight again."

"I guess it's a good thing they're around." This time when she pushed away, he didn't stop her.

Keith smirked and reached for the door handle. "Call me later."

"Maybe," Sedona said, teeth chattering, then turned and walked away.

Keith watched her and waited until she was halfway up the driveway before he shouted, "Sedona!"

She swung around and met his eyes. "Yes?"

"Merry Christmas, babe."

◆ ◆ ◆

Long after he was gone, Sedona sat out on the front porch deep in thought. In her lap was the gift Keith had given her, handmade by his mother's hands. *Creations by Cartwright* on the box with a Charlottesville address had hinted at such. When had he ordered them, she wondered? Shortly after they had started dating? She swallowed the lump of emotion in her throat and blinked away tears as she looked down at two miniature replicas of Cocoa made from wool roving with minimal hand stitching. Handcrafted for her tree for generations to come.

Keith had understood she was on the journey of starting her own tradition. A holiday tradition Sedona hoped to continue with a husband, and a family of her own. Something she wanted more than anything.

Sedona closed her eyes and drew cold air into her lungs. The only man she wanted a family with was Keith.

He was getting to her. As much as she wanted to deny it, she was dangling from the last shred of resistance. Her traitorous body refused to listen to her. It seemed impossible to shut off the emotions flowing through her heart. Sedona groaned as she stuffed her hands inside her coat pocket. Maybe if she didn't miss him so much, ignoring Keith would be much easier. Maybe if his apology didn't seem so sincere, extracting him from her life would be much simpler.

But he lied! He came into your life under false pretense, she kept trying to remind herself. And the even bigger question now was, what would Webb think? Would he approve of her dating Keith Falcon?

"Donie, what are you doing out here?"

She turned and looked at Dominique as she came out onto the porch wrapped in a long, beige trench coat. Instantly, Sedona's imagination went wild with the idea of showing up at Keith's doorstep wearing a similar one she had at home, hanging in her closet. Yet, instead of the creams slacks and green sweater, she would have shown up with nothing on underneath. Her body stirred. She definitely had it bad.

"It's so loud in there," she finally replied.

Dominique laughed. "Yes it is." The short, curvy woman took a seat beside Sedona on the wooden bench. "I had a chance to meet your friend. Very nice."

"Thanks." She put the box beside her.

Her sister-in-law turned on the seat and frowned. "Donie, why the long face?"

Sedona drew a breath and stared up into Dominique's eyes as she said, "I've been sitting out here asking myself, what would Webb think about me and Keith?"

Dominique had been a friend of the family long before she and Reese had started dating and she had been around Webb on several occasions.

"You think Webb wouldn't approve? I was only around your friend for a brief moment, but I got a good vibe around him."

Slowly, Sedona shook her head and said, "Keith and Webb were friends."

"What?"

She nodded. "Keith was on the ship when Webb died." Sedona was sure there was despair on her face because Dominique slid closer and rubbed a comforting hand up and down her arm.

"Wow! That's deep."

Nodding, her gaze shifted up toward the sunset. "They'd been friends for years. I just never put the connection together."

There was a pregnant pause. "How did you find out?"

"By chance, although, Keith had known all along. He just decided not to tell me." Sedona went on to tell her about finding the box of letters.

Dominique rubbed a hand across her short spiky hair and shook her head. "Oh girl! I need a box of popcorn, because this is definitely an ABC movie."

"Exactly." Sedona drew a sigh, allowing cool air to fill her lungs. "The story of my life."

Dominique's eyes studied her for a long moment. "How do you feel about him?"

"I think I'm in love with him," she said sadly.

"Oh Donie, that's fabulous!" She giggled, eyes bulging wide as they shared a look. Sedona could no longer resist a smile or the tears rolling down her cheek.

"Keith's really a wonderful man. I guess it's the fact he tried to deceive me that has me wondering if I have my head on right. If he lied to me about that, then what else could he possibly be lying about?" she explained and brushed the waterworks from her face.

The coffee-brown beauty frowned. "Does he give you reason to suspect he's hiding anything else?"

"No, but he didn't the first time either. I don't know." Feeling edgy and restless, Sedona rose then walked over and leaned against the porch railing. "I love the way I feel when I'm around him. Keith makes me laugh. The conversation is great. He's compassionate. Loving. A great kisser, and the sex is OMG!" She noted the warm shivers of delight at the memories.

Dominique blinked dark lashes over hopeful eyes. "Hey, that alone is enough of a reason not to let that man go."

"I know." In fact, Sedona missed everything about him. The way he checked on her every day. The way she slept in his arms with her head resting on his chest.

Dominique snapped her fingers in front of her face, drawing her from her reverie. "Donie, in order for you to have a shot at a real relationship with this man, you've got to find it in your heart to forgive."

Forgive. That's the problem. It had taken her forever to forgive Webb for dying. Now she had to find it in her heart to forgive Falcon for lying.

"I'm afraid," Sedona admitted with a long shaky breath.

Dominique eyed her with gentle concern. "Maybe *that's* the real problem."

Chapter 17

"We have all had an aha-moment. A time when we experience something that has a profound impact on how we see things, prompting us to make change."

Keith sat in the back row of the auditorium at the *A Brand New You* conference, being held at the Colgate Convention Center. He was listening to Sedona provide skills to men and women anxious to take both their personal and professional lives to the next level in the coming year.

"The key is to move beyond the moment and create long lasting change!"

Sedona was confident and powerful. Her body language and the level of knowledge had captured the attention of everyone in the auditorium, including him.

And he missed her like crazy.

In his bed, and in his life. Christmas had come and gone and he had yet to hear from her, so Keith decided it was time for him to take action.

After visiting Sedona's website, he saw she was doing a speaking engagement and book-signing as part of a holiday event, so Keith did something he hadn't done in years—he called in sick.

The room was packed. And when Keith finally saw Sedona saunter onto the stage, he'd felt an overwhelming sense of pride and possessiveness.

Mine.

She was brilliant, beautiful and she was his. He just needed to get her to see it.

"Aha!" she exclaimed drawing laughter from the crowd.

Keith scanned the audience and watched how engaged they were, listening to Sedona like a student to a professor. He admired the way she involved her audience, talking directly to them.

She was simply amazing.

As Keith watched her walk around the stage in a curve-hugging black dress, it was difficult to concentrate on what Sedona was saying. All he wanted to do was walk down to that stage, kiss her lips and run his fingers across her cheek.

He cleared his throat then shifted on the chair and tried again to stay focused. Keith watched as Sedona laughed, her eyes surveying the audience, looking for a show of hands. He willed her to look his way and when her eyes finally landed on his, Keith heard a short intake of breath through the microphone while his heart thudded beneath his chest. As he stared at Sedona, Keith felt as if time had stood still when in reality it had lasted barely a blink of the eye before she looked away. Sedona continued her speech, barely missing a beat, and he commended her on being a professional. Unfortunately, to his dismay, she made sure her eyes never shifted in his direction again.

The speaking engagement was followed by a book-signing. Keith got in line with the dozens of others and waited. He watched with interest the way Sedona personally greeted each of her fans with a warm smile and friendly chatter before personalizing their books. They didn't even seem to mind waiting for a chance to meet her in person.

When it was finally his turn, Keith stepped up to the table.

"Hello Donie."

Her head snapped up and he saw the spark in Sedona's eyes before she pushed it aside. Fine lines creased the skin around her eyes. "What are you doing here?"

"I came to see you in action," he explained and handed her the book he had purchased. "I'm very impressed."

"Well, thank you." There was no denying the longing in her eyes. "How would you like me to sign your book?"

He watched her lips that had been painted a soft coral pink. Her scent was something floral. Innocent. And distracting. "Anyway you like," he replied and Sedona smiled weakly.

She hesitated, reached for her pen and scribbled on the inside cover. "Here you go." She held the book out to him. "Thanks for coming and Happy New Year."

Keith leaned across the table and before Sedona could stop him, he pressed his lips to hers. As he withdrew, Keith met the startled look in her eyes as he whispered, "I love you, Sedona," before he turned and walked away.

◆ ◆ ◆

Did he just confess he loved me?

"Who was that?" Energi asked.

Sedona was ready to jump out of her seat and race after him, but she had a line of fans waiting. "That was Keith."

"Oh," she said and the tone in her voice indicated she knew how important he had become to her boss. On more than one occasion, her assistant had overheard the two of them on the phone.

Her eyes followed Keith as he walked down the hall until he was no longer in sight. Damn him! How dare he tell her he loved her and then walk away!

"Hi Ms. Beaumont, it's a pleasure to finally meet you."

She blinked, then brought her attention to the young man standing in front of her.

Sedona plastered on a smile and exchanged pleasantries. It took over an hour and the entire time she shifted restlessly thinking about the kiss followed by a wicked grin that made her breasts heavy and a pulse to start pounding at the apex of her thighs. How dare Keith tell her he love her and then walk away!

By the time the last book had been autographed, Sedona grabbed her iPhone and scurried into the other room and dialed Keith's number.

"Hey," he said and sounded like he was in bed. She could just see him laying across the bed in his naked glory.

"Did I wake you?"

"No, I was just...What can I help you with Sedona?"

His blunt response caught her off guard. "I..."What was wrong with her? "How dare you say what you said and then walk off?" she snapped.

There was a brief pause before Keith replied in a low baritone voice, "Tell me what I said Sedona."

She felt a flutter at the pit of her stomach. "You know what you said..., that stuff about loving me."

"That wasn't stuff. I do love you Sedona."

It was her turn to pause. "But...why?"

"Why?" There was a soft chuckle. "Why not? You're beautiful, funny, talented, sexy as hell. I love everything about you."

With an inward groan, Sedona realized Keith still wasn't playing fair. "I told you I needed time," she said on a rough sigh, dragging a hand across the back of her neck.

Keith paused and Sedona held her breath, waiting with uncertainty. "Take all the time you need. No offense, but a man can only take so much rejection," he added with a humorless chuckle. "I love you, Sedona, and I want to spend the rest of my life with you, but you have to want the same. You're gonna have to let me know you want me. In the meantime, enjoy the rest of your holiday and Happy New Year's."

Her head was swimming. She didn't know what to say except, "Okay."

And then the phone went dead.

♦ ♦ ♦

Keith moved across his townhouse, carrying a Christmas card over to the fireplace and placed it on top of the mantel. His mother had sent it to him. Inside was a smiling photo of her, her husband George and their cat Snowball.

Going to see Sedona today and then telling her he loved her had been a bold move, but he was starting to get desperate. Unfortunately, the day hadn't turned out at all like he had envisioned.

Keith guessed he had expected his own aha-moment.

While crossing the room, he stopped and stood behind a large armchair. His fingers pressed into the padding of its high leather back as he stared over at the book on the coffee table that Sedona hadn't bothered to personalize and simply autographed, *All the best, Sedona.*

It felt like a pie to his face.

Keith had been so irritated that as soon as he'd left the convention center, he had gone home, changed into a running suit, and drove to the gym a few blocks away. He needed to clear his head and lifting weights was the only thing he could think of that worked, but after a while he realized it was a waste of time. There was only one thing that could fix what ailed him and that was Sedona.

His thoughts raced nonstop. Hours and days had passed and he'd been operating on nothing but coffee. He couldn't sleep, he barely remembered to eat. All he could think about was Sedona and that he might have lost her. It was so bad, Keith was actually looking forward to going into work in the morning. He desperately needed the distraction and work was something that required his undivided attention. But at the end of the day he would be back at home, watching his phone, waiting for the call that never came.

Keith scowled and headed down the hall to shower. He stepped into the adjoining bathroom, turned on the water, then stripped his clothes. Once he was under the spray of the water, his thoughts consumed him again.

The only woman he wanted was Sedona.

What if she never forgives you?

The thought sickened him, and he refused to believe it. Sedona loved him. He'd seen it in her eyes. He'd heard it in her voice. Yep, what they had wasn't over. She asked for time to think and that was exactly what he planned to give her.

He would continue to wait although it wasn't going to be easy. Patience had never been one of his strong points.

Chapter 18

On New Year's Eve, Sedona was seated at one of her favorite seafood restaurants in Cape Martin, waiting for Victoria Webb to arrive.

Outside the snow was starting to come down, painting the street a beautiful white, a dramatic contrast to the festive decorations of red and gold adoring the streets. The small town reminded her so much of Main Street in Sheraton Beach with its quaint shops and Mom & Pop stores. Wreathes were on storefront doors and light poles had been striped like candy canes with garland. Normally, she behaved like a little girl in a toy store, but this holiday season she didn't give a damn about any of it.

Did I make a mistake?

Before she saw Keith at the convention center, he'd been sending her daily text messages. **Good morning. Hope you have an amazing day. Thinking of you.** All in which she had ignored. But now, ever since the book signing, she hadn't heard a word from him. She found herself watching her phone, checking for messages every five minutes, but it had been almost three days and nothing. Panic clawed at her chest. Had Keith finally given up? The sad thing was she didn't want him to. She wanted him to continue to pursue her and try to wear her down, until finally she surrendered, but apparently he was a man of his word.

You're gonna have to let me know you want me.

In all honesty, there was nothing she wanted more than Keith.

Yes, he had lied to her but did it really matter anymore? She blew a deep sigh of despair. She was starting to lose her mind. Last night she had called Keith several times, but he never answered. Sedona had even texted that she wanted to talk and needed to see him, and yet, still nothing. And now she had a scary feeling it was too late. Men like Keith didn't just sit around waiting for a woman to come to her senses. If anything he'd already found a woman more willing and had moved on. Sickened at the thought, she pressed a hand to her queasy stomach and prayed it wasn't too late.

"I'm here!"

She looked up as Victoria Webb sauntered toward her looking beautiful in a long pink wool coat. Sedona rose and tilted her chin as the sixty-two-year-old kissed her cheek. The smell of her expensive perfume invaded her mind.

"So good to see you!" Sedona said and wrapped her arms around the little woman. She had often joked about how could someone so petite have given birth to such a large son.

"Good to see you, too. Sorry I'm late," she said apologetically. She removed the scarf from around her neck and touched an elegant hand to her coiffed, graying hair, brushing away snowflakes. "It was extra busy at the B&B, but I had no idea it would take me this long to get away." She went on to explain as she lowered into the chair beside her. Victoria and her husband Arnie managed Charlotte's Webb, a large farmhouse bed & breakfast with gorgeous views of the Chesapeake Bay named after Arnie's mother.

Sedona gave her a dismissive wave. "No worries.

Thanks for inviting me to come up. I desperately needed to get out the house today."

Victoria's amber eyes searched her face as she smiled. "Thank you for coming, my dear. I've really missed you."

"I missed you too." They shared a smile. "Actually, I was sitting here enjoying the view of the town. It's like a winter wonderland!" she added with a flick of her wrist.

Victoria looked out the picture window and beamed. "Yes, the town went all out this year. I think it has something to do with that new female mayor we have. Arnie and I are attending the New Year's party this evening. You should come."

And spend New Year's Eve alone? No way.

"No, I need to get back to Hampton before the snow gets too heavy. I just really wanted to see you and bring you your Christmas present." With that said, Sedona reached inside her purse and removed a pink card, Victoria's signature color.

"Splendid, because I have something for you as well!" Victoria cried and then signaled for the waiter.

While they ordered Sedona noticed the snow had begun to come down even heavier.

"How have you been?" Victoria asked after their waiter went to get their waters and basket of bread.

"To be honest…, I'm finally ready to move on with my life."

"Dear, that is excellent news! You are too beautiful to waste away. My son would have wanted that."

Yes, Webb would have. She was really starting to believe that.

"Now you need to get out there and meet yourself a nice young man."

Webb's mother looked so worried that Sedona heard

herself blurting out, "I met someone."

Victoria's eyes sparkled with intrigue. "Really? Tell me more."

She shrugged. "The jury is still out on our relationship."

"I can tell by the twinkle in your eyes, whoever he is, he's someone special."

"Yes, he is." So if that was the case why had it been so hard for her to look past the deception and forgive? "I want a relationship like you and Mr. Arnie."

Victoria gave a rude snort. "Mr. Arnie is in the dog house. He forgot the name of my favorite perfume and bought something I never heard of for our anniversary. I think that man is starting to get senile."

Sedona chuckled and the waiter returned with their clam chowder. She loved the stories Webb used to tell of his parents first meeting while in kindergarten when his father poured watercolor paint in his mother's hair.

While they ate, they chatted some more.

"I am so glad you decided to finally come up and visit me," Victoria said and dabbed at the corner of her mouth with the linen napkin.

"I know. I feel so bad it has taken me so long." Almost a year to be exact since she had come up to see them and to put flowers on Webb's grave.

"You have to come and visit me more often. I know how much you love the seafood here. This restaurant is so popular, in fact, I meet a friend of mine here every year around this time, but so far nothing. Oh well…, how's work been?"

"I've been great. Work is really booming."

"That is wonderful, not that I am surprised. You were always smart. I knew you were going to make me some beautiful, smart grandbabies."

Sedona smiled as she continued eating her soup. She had always adored Webb's parents. They had a natural way of making people feel welcome.

"Arnie wanted to join you, but there's some game on television he didn't want to miss," she explained.

Sedona giggled. "You'll just have to say hello to Mr. Arnie for me."

"I—" Victoria stopped and her attention shifted across the restaurant. "Oh, here comes that friend of mine now."

Sedona looked over toward the hostess station and her heart picked up tempo when she spotted Keith coming their way. What was he doing here? she wondered. Eyes filled with confusion she turned and met Victoria's gaze as she gave her a sly smirk.

"Actually Keith's more like a son than a good friend," she added with a wink.

Did she know?

Sedona was flabbergasted as she watched Victoria rise from the chair, smiling as he approached.

"Keith, dear."

"Sorry I'm late, Mrs. Webb." He wrapped his arms around her and placed a kiss to her cheek. When he drew back, Victoria stared up at Keith adoringly. The same way she used to look at her son.

Now both were staring at her.

"Sedona, I would like you to meet Keith."

She rose and their eyes locked, causing her body to throb with need.

He was the first to hold out his hand. "Hello, Sedona. I'm Keith Falcon. It's a pleasure to finally meet you. Webb talked a lot about you."

She played along. "Oh yes. We met briefly at his funeral. He talked a lot about you as well." She took his hand and intense heat engulfed her chest on contact.

They returned to their seats and Keith lowered onto the chair on the right side of her.

"I'm so glad to finally get the two of you together. I've wanted to do this for a long while," Victoria explained, merrily.

Sedona caught Keith looking at her, and her entire body came to life. Was she dreaming or was Keith really here? From under the table she had to pinch herself just to be sure.

Victoria went into a spill about Webb and Keith serving together and all the times he'd come to Cape Martin to check on her and Arnie since his death. Sedona studied Keith's face. Why hadn't he told her?

The waiter brought Keith a bowl of soup and while they ate, she stared across the table at him. Memories tugged at her of the last few weeks they had spent together. All the joy Keith had brought into her life in such a short period of time.

She loved him. It was funny but she could barely remember why she had been angry. All she knew was this was the man she wanted to spend the rest of her life with, if he'd still have her. As she watched him, she saw all the emotions stirring in his eyes some she didn't recognize and then there were the feelings that mirrored her own.

Suddenly, she put down her spoon, and whispered, "I love you."

Someone gasped and she wasn't sure if it was Keith or Victoria.

Keith swung around on his chair. "Did you just say you love me?"

Sedona took a deep, steadying breath and nodded with tears in her eyes.

A grin curled Keith's lips as he reached under the table and took her hand in his. "Forgive me, Mrs. Webb. I already know Sedona. In fact, I'm in love with her," he explained.

"Is that so?"

Sedona stole a nervous glance in her direction and noticed Victoria looked confused.

"He's right. We met weeks ago." Sedona then went on to explain how they had met online.

"Only I didn't tell her who I was," Keith blurted and Sedona's eyes widened, surprised at his openness, and then she smiled.

"Of course, I eventually figured out the truth. And never wanted to see him again."

Victoria frowned. "Keith shame on you. Why did you lie?"

He turned to Sedona and stared, searching the depths of her eyes as he said, "From the second I saw Sedona I knew I wanted her in my life and I wanted a real shot, but I was afraid my relationship with Webb was gonna keep me from having her."

Victoria's elbow was on the table, chin resting in her palm, amusement tickling her lips as she listened and observed.

It was Sedona's turn to smile. "I told him I never wanted to see him again, but Keith refused to take no for an answer."

"Because I know who I want."

It appeared a light went on in Victoria's eyes, and she suddenly snapped her manicured fingers. "So that's why after all these years of asking you to meet Sedona, you finally agreed."

His eyes were on Sedona when he nodded. "Yes. I needed an excuse to see her."

Victoria started laughing "This is working out far better than I had imagined it would! Wait until I tell Arnie. Derrick would have been so happy."

Keith reached over and laced his fingers with her. "You hear that, Donie? Webb would have approved of us."

Sedona nodded while blinking away tears. "Yes, I believe he would have."

They only had eyes for each other.

"I love you," he mouthed.

"I love you, too," she whispered as her heart swelled with love and admiration.

Victoria cleared her throat. "Well, I hate to leave you two, but Arnie just called and he needs help at the B&B." She rose and swung the purse over her shoulder. "I hope the two of you change your mind and decide to stick around for the celebration tonight. If you do, they'll be a room at the B&B waiting for you."

Gazing at Victoria, Sedona saw the smile on her lips and the tears pooling her amber eyes. She rose and put her arms around her. "He's a good one. Don't you dare let him get away," she whispered.

"I won't," Sedona replied and then released her.

"Good. I might get those grandbabies after all."

Victoria dropped a kiss to Keith's cheek. He whispered something in her ear that sounded like, thank you. And then she was gone before Keith could grab his coat and walk her to the door.

"I don't remember hearing her phone ring," Sedona said with amusement.

Keith chuckled. "Neither do I. I think she was busy matchmaking."

"I'm glad she did."

Keith stroked her cheek, gazing at her tenderly. "So

am I." Reaching for her hand again, Keith brought it to his lips and kissed it. "I missed you."

Sedona brought a hand up to frame his face. "And I missed you." They were staring at each other when their waiter arrived to clear away the soup bowls.

"Are you ready for me to take your order?" he asked with his pen and pad ready.

Keith's brow rose as he looked to Sedona. "Are you hungry?"

She shook her head. "Not anymore."

Within moments he had the bill settled. They bundled into their coats and she tied the scarf around her neck and took Keith's hand as he led her out the restaurant. The snow was coming down heavier. It was thick, white and beautiful. Tilting her head back, Sedona caught a snowflake on her tongue. Something about walking like this, with him, was deeply peaceful.

"Looks like you're getting a white New Year's."

"I'll take it." Despite the snow the wind was still. It was a perfect winter night for walking and cuddling up in front of a wood fire.

"Donie, spend New Year's with me."

Her heart thumped. "I would love to. Do you have any plans in particular?"

"A little birdie told me there's a party going on at the banquet hall tonight."

"Is that so?" she teased. "Okay, sounds like fun, but I don't have anything to wear?"

"Take your pick. I'm sure we can find something at one of these boutiques." He squeezed her hand. "I came prepared."

She stopped walking and stared up at him. "You knew?"

"I hoped you would want to stay," Keith whispered

unevenly.

With a nod, Sedona's eyes filled with tears. "I can't breathe without you," she murmured.

Keith tugged her into his arms, then leaned down and kissed her. Her mouth parted beneath his and Sedona marveled at the familiar sensation. She met his hunger with her own, feasting on his lips, her arms locked around his neck. Keith held her tightly against him. It had been too long.

They slowly drew apart and Keith smiled into her eyes and said, "Are you ready to go shopping?"

Sedona shook her head. "No. I rather go check in over at the B&B. A little birdie told me a room will be waiting for us."

He tossed his head back with hearty laughter. "Sweetheart, your every wish is my desire."

Keith scooped her into his arms and captured Sedona's lips in a kiss that was so powerful it left her breathless.

THE BEAUMONT SERIES

The Second Time Around

The Playboy's Proposition

The Player's Proposal

For You I Do

Before I Let You Go

Every Second Counts

A Beau for Christmas

Do Me Baby

Breathless

Enjoy a sneak peak of

Can't Put a Price Tag on Love

~~The Campbells~~

Prologue

Martin Campbell stepped into his room and discovered a sweet little thing waiting on his bed.

"Hey, I've been waiting for you," she cooed.

He couldn't respond because the words had been sucked clearly from his lungs. Instead, all he could do was stare.

Curly reddish-brown hair tumbled loose and wild around her shoulders. The lamp on the bedside table sent gleams of light across her pert nose and high cheekbones. Large gray eyes sparkled with excitement. But he was a man, and her face wasn't at all what he was focused on. He couldn't have stopped looking even if he had wanted to. Not with her lying across his bed in a see-through white teddy with matching panties. The tantalizing outfit showcased every last curve. Even now, looking at her made his mouth dry. She had a body that was hazardous to his health and needed to be labeled SIN. The whole scenario was sending strong sexual signals to his brain. He would have welcomed his little surprise with open arms, but the honey was barely sixteen.

"Come on in." Her sweet voice and enticing smile startled him, forcing him to take a deep breath to maintain control.

Remembering his parents were right down the hall, Martin eased the door shut and moved over near the bed. "What in the world are you doing here?" he asked in a stern whisper.

"I was waiting for you." Her wide eyes revealed a blend of wariness and bravado.

"For what?" Martin snapped. It was almost midnight. What would his parents think if they found her in his bed half-naked? "Candy, you need to get to Chenoa's room, *now*." She was supposed to be spending the night with his sister, not him.

She shook her head. "No, I've something to tell you." Watching him with fearful intensity, she sat up straighter, pushing her young breasts against the thin material. "Something important."

"We can talk in the morning." It took considerable effort to focus only on her face.

"No, I want to talk now." She said reminding him of a spoiled brat.

He raked a hand across his thick curls then said in a weary voice, "What do you want to talk about?" he asked, then watched her take another deep breath.

"I want you to make love to me."

Good Lord, he was lusting over a little girl. It took everything he had to say, "You need to put your clothes on and get out of my room."

"Why?" she said in a sugary, un-Candy like voice that played havoc with his imagination. "I love you and want you to take my virginity."

He watched the way her breasts bounced as she spoke. *Man it was hard being twenty-two.* In a firm big brother tone, Martin said, "Candy. I'm way too old for you. Save your virginity for someone special. Save that for the right man. Now get out of my room before my parents find you here."

She scooted backward against the pillow and dragged her knees to her chest. "Stop treating me like a child. I'm a woman now."

Yes, you are, he thought as he took another long look. All the more reason for him to get her out of his room *fast*. "You're sixteen. I'm twenty-two. I don't know if you know this, but there is this thing called rape."

"Not if I consent," she added defiantly.

He shook his head, incredulously. "Legally, you're too young to consent."

Candace shifted on the bed enough for him to catch a glimpse of her right buttock. *Good, Lord*. Somehow he was going to have to find a way to talk some sense into her head before he ended up doing something they would both later regret. He reached across the bed for her hand. "Okay, games over. It's late and I've got a long day tomorrow."

"I'm not here to play games." Candace regarded him with that curious aura of seductress and schoolgirl. She then drew in a deep breath and with a dramatic sweep of her arm, dropped her legs. "Please, Martin. My mother said save my virginity for the man I love and planned to marry. Well, that man is you!"

He stood, paralyzed, his hand outstretched and his mind in the gutter. She was lying there with her legs open and her thighs parted wide. Martin licked his lips as he took it all in. If only he could climb onto that bed, push the crotch of her panties aside and taste her —

Forcing a laugh, he pushed the ludicrous thoughts aside. "What you have is a case of puppy love. Next month you'll be in love with someone else," he replied, sounding surprisingly calm for a man whose groin was screaming at him.

"No I won't. I'll never love anyone but you," Candace said with theatrical passion. She slid out of bed to stand before him, and already he felt the treacherous flutter in his stomach. "Now that you're leaving for college tomorrow, I felt you should know how I feel," she recited in a rush. "I've loved you from the moment I first came to your house. Even though I never said it before, I do love you."

"Whatever," he muttered under his breath trying to hide the arousal her confession had stirred. "You're much too young to know what real love is."

"I know my own heart," she said, her voice quivering a little. "Please, let me show you how much I love you." She threw herself at him so unexpectedly, he fell back onto his futon with its loads of clean clothes he had yet to put away. By instinct, he caught her in his arms. Her soft breasts made a cushion against his chest providing him with the forbidden warmth of an adolescent. Quickly, he pushed her away. "Candy, the answer is no. I'm engaged to Tamara."

"I don't like her," she declared, her chin held at a defiant tilt as she stood over him.

Martin chuckled impatiently. "You don't have to like her."

"Chenoa and Chante don't like her either."

Obviously his two sisters have been talking about him behind his back again. "I am not about to discuss my love life with you. I'm sorry but Tamara's a woman and you are a child. I don't seduce little girls."

"Do I look like a little girl," she insisted. Candy kept her determined gaze trained on him as her slim fingers plucked at her nipples. Sweat broke out on his brow. He could see their fullness through the material, their taut peaks. For one mad moment, his other head controlled his logic. He wanted to see her naked, to kiss her senseless, to tumble down onto the sheets and sink into her hot, tight —.

Snatching a sweatshirt from the futon, he tossed it at her. "Cover yourself."

Candace clutched the garment to her chest. "But Chenoa said you wouldn't be able to resist me if I wore this outfit."

"My sister lied," he said through gritted teeth. He should have known his little sister was the mastermind behind this charade. Where in the world did she find such an outfit in the first place?

Tears swam in the eyes that gazed down at him. "I do love you. Why can't you see that?"

"Because you're like a little sister to me. Now go." Martin grabbed Candy's arm and propelled her toward the door. "Do me a favor and don't ever do anything like this again."

Candace dug in her bare heels. With a stubborn fierceness, she turned on him. "You are making a big mistake. Tamara is gonna break your heart. She will never love you the way I will."

"Tamara loves me, otherwise she wouldn't have accepted my proposal."

Her unruly red hair rippled around her shoulders. "The only reason why she wants to be your wife is because she thinks you have a shot at getting picked up by one of those pro teams."

"No it's not," he snapped then raked a frustrated hand through his hair. "Listen, Candy, you're a sweet girl, but that's it. I love Tammy."

The glimpse of pain in her eyes, bothered him more than he expected. The last thing he wanted to do was to hurt such a sweet kid. "Candy. I'm crazy about you, but you're like a sister to me. The last thing I would ever want to do is ruin our friendship."

"But I don't want to be your friend. I want to be your

wife," she pouted.

Goodness, she doesn't know when quit. He had to put an end to this silliness once and for all. "It will never happen," he said harshly. "Even if I wasn't engaged I would never be interested in you."

She flinched, her lower lip quivering. The wounded look in her eyes was almost more than he could bear. On a choked sob, she tossed the sweatshirt back at him. "I hate you, Martin Alexander Campbell. You go ahead and go to college and marry that chicken-head Tamara. And when she dumps you, don't say I didn't tell you so!" Then she darted out of the room and down the hall to Chenoa's room on the end.

Martin leaned against door and took a heavy breath. How in the world was he now supposed to sleep with her sweet feminine scent flooding the air? He liked Candy and hated that he had to reject her. It bothered him that he hurt her feelings, but even more, he despised himself for desiring her. Pushing away the thought, he moved over to his bed and prepared to go to sleep. Some day Candy would thank him for saving her from her own foolishness.

Chapter One

Ten years later

Candace Price stood in front of the gravesite shielded from the warm sun by a large blue awning. Her sister's head was resting on her shoulder, their arms wrapped about each other's waist, offering comfort. As she listened to the minister's bland intonation, she was quiet trying to stare at the vast array of flower arrangements around them and not down at the open grave or the coffin waiting to be lowered into the ground.

This moment reminded her too much of being eighteen again. Vibrant, full of life and so looking forward to going away to college. She had been offered a full scholarship to Purdue University. Her parents were so excited because she would have been the first person in their family to have gone to college. In honor of her accomplishment, her good friend Chenoa, and her family, the Campbell's, had given her a party. Coconut cake, homemade black walnut ice cream, ribs so tender they were falling off the bones, and Mama Campbell's to-die-for potato salad. Candace blinked the tears away from her eyes. She remembered it like it was just yesterday. Because it had also been the day her parents were killed by a hit and run driver.

Shanice's hold tightened as if she had read her big sister's mind. Candace was certain her sister, too, was remembering their parents. Who could forget? For her graduation present, her parents had bought her a temperamental VW Bug. Her mother had insisted that Shanice go on to the party with Candace and they would catch up as soon as they dropped by the hardware store to pick up a new faucet for the kitchen sink. An hour later, her parents were dead. She thanked God every day that he hadn't taken her sister's life that day as well.

Blinking, she returned her mind to the present and listened to the minister's closing words. They lowered the coffin into the ground, and Candace stepped back, watching in disbelief. She still couldn't believe that Sheila was dead. It was unreal. She had just seen her last week while visiting Shanice on campus and now she was dead. It had been ruled a drug overdose. Candace still hadn't digested the possibility that sweet little Sheila had been taking drugs.

Her eyes traveled over to the parents, both distraught, sitting in the front row in tears. She had never liked funerals and since her parents' tragic death she hadn't attended a single one. But Sheila had been her sister's roommate and when Shanice called, she rushed to Columbia. Once again she saw it as her responsibility to comfort her.

Family, students and faculty murmured their condolences; their voices blended into a quiet, indecipherable stirring in the air. Shanice released her. Candace stared down at her. Several wisps of her auburn hair escaped her ponytail. She pushed them away from her face and gave her sister a slight smile.

"I'm gonna go say something to Sheila's parents." Tears rimmed her amber eyes and droplets hung from her long thick lashes. Candace nodded, then watched the dejected sag of Shanice's shoulders as she shuffled her feet across the grass. She stood back and waited, wanting to give them their privacy and allowed them a moment to hug and together say good-bye. The girls had been roommates for almost two years.

Candace slipped her sunglasses over her eyes and headed toward her sister who looked anxious to leave. Arm and arm they walked over to her beat up Corolla and climbed in. They were quiet as they left the cemetery. She drove several miles before Shanice reached over and turned on 106.1. Chris Brown's voice filled the air.

She sneaked a peak at her sister. "You want to go and get something to eat?" she suggested.

Staring out the window, Shanice shook her head.

An awkward moment of silence passed before Candace cleared her throat and tried again. "How about coming with me and staying at Tia's house?"

"No, I'd rather just go home." Weariness had crept into her voice.

"Okay, well, I can sleep in —"

"I really want to be alone, "Shanice replied, declining her offer to spend the night with her. She closed her eyes briefly then opened them again. "Candy, I'm sorry. I'm just tired and very irritable. I really just want to be by myself."

"I understand."

"How about we have breakfast in the morning before you head home?"

Candace glanced over and smiled. "Sounds like a plan."

After she dropped Shanice off at her apartment, Candace headed south of town. The day was gloomy just like her mood. Overcast skies, crisp cool wind blowing, rain was definitely in the forecast. She drove down Providence Road past the Mizzou's new football stadium, constructed by donations from the University's rich alumni. She liked the small college town and was intending to move from St. Louis just as soon as she could land herself a job on campus. That way she could keep a closer eye on her little sister.

Candace drove until the road ended, then made a right and turned into a fabulous new subdivision where her good friend, Tia Rose, lived. The two had met one summer while away at camp and had been friends ever since. She pulled in front of the newly constructed two-story home. The landscapers were out front laying sod in her yard. Tia was standing on the porch watching.

Moving up the driveway, she took in her long, dark-brown locks that complemented her heart-shaped face. Even from a distance she could see the three carat diamond sparkling on her left hand. After a five year engagement, the bookstore owner was finally getting married in November.

When she reached the porch, Tia gave her a look of concern. "Where's Shanice?"

"She went home. She wanted to be alone."

Tia gave her a knowing look, then signaled for her to follow her inside. Candace stepped into the foyer where an elegant chandelier hung overhead and moved through the scarcely furnished house to the kitchen. Stainless steel appliances, pot-racks hanging over a large cherry wood island and lots and lots of windows; it was any woman's dream.

"Have a seat. You hungry?" Tia asked as she walked over to the refrigerator.

Shaking her head, she moved over to the island and pulled out a matching stool, then took a seat. "No, not really."

"Then at least have something to drink." She carried over a pitcher of fresh lemonade and moved to retrieve two glasses.

"How was the funeral?" Tia asked while pouring them both something to drink.

"Like all funerals. Depressing. Lot of crying. Shanice was like a zombie through the entire thing. She is really taking Sheila's death hard." She paused and blew out a frustrated breath. "I don't know what to do to cheer her up."

"All you can do is be there for her. People have to grieve in their own way." She had a faraway look in her eyes and she knew that she was thinking about her father who had died from liver failure two years ago.

"Well enough about that depressing stuff. We have a wedding to plan."

Her face lit up at the mention of her fiancé.

"Why don't you just get married on one of your brother-in-law's cruise ships?

Tia shook her head. "As much I loved Charity's wedding, I want to do something different, unique maybe."

During her ten-year class reunion, Charity had reunited with her classmate and they were married six months later. "What about the Shelter Gardens?"

Frowning, she shook her head. "No, everyone has done that. We have to think of something else."

"I know," she said with a snap of her finger. "Let's go to the Expo next weekend."

"Ooh! That's a good idea. Where're they having it?"

"It's going to be in St. Charles this year. Last year they had a huge wedding show. Models, vendors, you name it."

"That's sound like a plan. I'll even spend the night with you. Maybe we can go out."

"I haven't been clubbing in a while. Usually it's the

same old thing, old pop-pops or a bunch of thugs with their pants hanging off their butts."

"Well, we need to work on finding you a husband."

Candace snorted rudely. "A man is the last thing I need."

"No, a man is exactly what you need. Don't you get lonely?"

"Yeah, that's why I bought myself a cat."

"A cat can't keep you warm at night. You need to find someone special like your good friend, Chenoa, and what's her husband's name?"

"Zearl. Zearl Sinclair."

"Yeah, Zearl," she repeated with a dreamy smile. "I love that name. How's the baby?"

"Anasia is doing fabulous. I'm flying down in August for her first birthday. I can't wait."

"You're sure it's not her uncle Martin that you can't wait to see."

She dropped her face, hoping that Tia didn't see her blush. "Don't be ridiculous. Martin and I are just friends."

"Keep saying that. I remembered the way you talked about him at camp that summer."

"I was only sixteen at the time."

"True but you still have that same look in your eyes, even now when you talk about him."

"Girl, quit playing."

"Who's playing?" She met her eyes. "Look, you're still in love with him. I don't know why you keep trying to deny it."

Candace took a long sip and considered denying her feelings even longer but what was the point. She needed to share her feelings about him with someone. "You're right. I do still love him. I've loved him for as long as I can remember."

"Well, now that you're both grown you should tell him."

"It wouldn't work."

"Why?"

"I didn't tell you this, but last summer when we attended Chante's engagement party, that's Chenoa's older sister, Martin and I went out and um...we kissed."

"What! And you didn't tell me. Well, what happened?"

"Nothing happened. We went out. We kissed and then his girlfriend showed up."

While she finished her lemonade, she told her she had bought the perfect little black dress and after years of yearning, she had finally gotten Martin's attention. After dinner he had taken her back to his house where they kissed. That might have led to more if it hadn't been for his gold-digging girlfriend Valerie, who had popped up in nothing but high heels and a trench coat, looking for a lil' somethin' somethin'. She had waited almost a decade to feel his lips pressed to hers and it had been worth the wait. "The kiss meant nothing to him. He took me back to his sister's and we haven't spoken since." She remembered sitting around watching her phone that never rang with his number on the caller ID. "I saw him at Chante's wedding last fall. He tried to talk to me but I pretended I was too busy."

"How long are you gonna keep playing these games? If you want that man you better go and get him."

"It's too much work. I don't have the time or the patience."

"You need to find the time."

"Relationships are just too much work and I guess I am just too selfish to put in that much effort."

"Well, we're going to change all that. I'll be down in two weeks, and we are going to hit the town. Jerold will be so jealous." She giggled playfully. "I've got to stir things up every now and then, otherwise men start to take you for granted."

"Oh really?"

"Really."

♦ ♦ ♦

"Sorry Mr. Campbell, hospital rules."

Martin slumped back in the seat and watched as the elevator doors closed. It was no use arguing. It was embarrassing enough as it is that he'd been shot in the butt. Now he was being pushed through the hospital lobby in a wheelchair.

"Who's picking you up?" he heard his nurse ask.

"My brother Dame." He scowled at the thought. If anyone else was available, Dame would have been the last person he would have called. And he could already hear the jokes and was not at all looking forward to it. He would have preferred to just drive himself home and his family never know he had come into the emergency room this evening, but unfortunately per hospital rules, he could not drive himself home.

The elevator doors opened and she pushed him out and hit a bump. He gritted his teeth against the pain.

"Sorry about that," she said apologetically. "We're almost there."

He waited until the pain subsided, then took a deep breath and shifted lightly trying to ease some of the pressure. While they moved down the hall he could feel everyone looking at him and wondering what had happened.

"All right. As we move through the double doors there might be a small bump," she warned.

He braced himself and was happy when the wheelchair finally came to a halt.

"Okay, we've made it." Nurse Bryant said with a smile as she moved around to the side so that he could see her.

Martin gave a smile that felt plastic. What in the world did he need to be happy about? He was on an indefinite leave of absence following a humiliating accident that should have never happened

She pushed a blonde strand of hair away from her face and then asked, "How long have you been a cop?"

Too long was what he wanted to say. But it was his whole life. Without his job what else was there for him to do? "For about six years now."

"Wow! My grandfather was with the Philadelphia Police Department for over twenty years. It was all he knew."

It was all he knew as well. Being on leave was going to be hard and possibly next to impossible.

He heard heavy bass system bumping coming from a distance. It wasn't long before he spotted an Impala pulling up in the circular driveway. Twenty inch rims. Tinted windows and a fresh metallic green paint job. Out came his brother Dame.

"Whassup, big bro!" Dame chuckled as he moved around to where Martin was waiting.

Rolling his eyes, Martin gave him a dismissive wave. The jokes were only seconds away.

Nurse Bryant gave him a warm smile. "How about you get the door open and you can help me get him in the car."

"No problem. No problem at all." He watched as his

brother tried to hide his smirk as he moved and opened the passenger side door.

"I can walk."

"Are you sure? Yo, Marty, you sure you don't need no help?"

"I said I'm fine," he snapped. He didn't mean to seem ungrateful but this situation was embarrassing enough as it was. Slowly he pushed up out of the chair with Nurse Bryant standing by just in case he needed her. The pain was excruciating but there was no way he was going to let them know that.

He brushed back tears as he stood up tall. Then took one step and another ten until he reached the door.

"Wait before you sit down. Don't forget your inflatable donut."

Dame chuckled. "Yo, you definitely don't want to forget that."

Martin gave him an evil stare and waited until Nurse Bryant put the donut on the seat before he moved and slowly lowered himself on top of it.

Standing right outside the window, Nurse Bryant signaled for him to roll it down. "I hope you feel better. All your instructions are in the bag and we'll see you in a few weeks to check your wound site." She waved goodbye and Dame pulled away. Silence filled the car, but Martin could tell he was trying to hold it in.

"Go ahead. I know you want to laugh."

Dame exploded. "Sorry bro, but you have to admit this is funny."

"Ha-ha. Very funny."

"My bad, Marty, when you called I thought you were joking," he said between chuckles as he stopped at a red light.

He groaned. "I just want to get home and take some

more pain killers. Do me a favor and don't tell mom about this."

"Oops, my bad."

"My bad? Don't tell me you called her."

"I've got to work in the morning and figured you'd need someone to help you."

He groaned. "Thanks a lot." Dame was a motor mouth. He would never live it down. The last thing he wanted was for the entire family to know he'd been shot in the butt by a nine-year-old kid.

Coming in 2016

THE CAMPBELLS

Love Uncovered

When I First Saw You

Can't Put a Price Tag on Love (2016)

Other Books by Angie Daniels

Feinin' *Big Spankable Asses Anthology*
Tease
Seduced into Submission
Talk A Good Game
When It Rains
Love Uncovered
When I First Saw You
In the Company of My Sistahs
Trouble Loves Company
Careful of the Company You Keep
Intimate Intentions
Hart & Soul
Time is of the Essence
A Will to Love
Endless Enchantment
Destiny In Disguise
The Second Time Around
The Playboy's Proposition
The Player's Proposal
For You I Do
Before I Let You Go
In Her Neighbor's Bed
Show Me
Any Man Will Do
Coming for My Baby
Strutting in Red Stilettos
Running to Love in Pink Stilettos
Say My Name
Every Second Counts
A Beau for Christmas
Do Me Baby
Naughty Before Christmas
Curious- Seduced into Submission
Served- Seduced into Submission
Time for Pleasure
For Her Pleasure
Beg For It
Put Your Name on It

ABOUT THE AUTHOR

Angie Daniels is a free spirit who isn't afraid to say what's on her mind or even better, write about it. Since strutting onto the literary scene in five-inch heels, she's been capturing her audience's attention with her wild imagination and love for alpha men. The *USA Today* Bestselling Author has written over twenty-five novels for imprints such as BET Arabesque, Harlequin/Kimani Romance and Kensington/ Dafina and Kensington/Aphrodisia Books. For more information about upcoming releases, and to connect with Angie on Facebook, please visit her website at www.angiedaniels.com.

Made in the USA
San Bernardino, CA
16 September 2016